MURDER IN A WATCHED ROOM

A.G. BARNETT

ODDMOOR PRESS

MAILING LIST

G et FREE SHORT STORY *A Rather Inconvenient Corpse* by signing up to the mailing list at agbarnett.com

CHAPTER ONE

Brock watched with folded arms as Detective Sergeant Guy Poole paced up and down in front of him. The dimly lit street shimmered as the light drizzle slanted across it, as though someone had smudged the world with oil. He tore his gaze away and surveyed the surrounding buildings, looking again for any sign of CCTV cameras, but he knew there were none.

This side street saw little foot traffic, they had to hope that some of the other residents in the block of flats had seen something, but his years of experience told him that people were strangely deaf, dumb and blind when it came to witnessing crimes. Assuming there had been anything to see here. They didn't even know if anything had happened here yet.

Poole stopped his meandering as movement

stirred in the doorway of the building. Sheila Hopkins appeared in her familiar white suit and Poole dashed towards her.

"Anything?" he asked desperately as Detective Inspector Sam Brock came up behind him.

"I'm sorry love, we couldn't find anything out of the ordinary. We've taken a load of prints, but let's not get our hopes up." She shrugged. They all knew that whoever had taken Poole's mother was likely to have worn gloves.

Poole nodded and turned away.

Brock exchanged a look of concern with Sheila, who squeezed his arm before heading away to her van.

Brock watched as his young partner wandered aimlessly along the dark street in front of him. Just hours ago they had been with friends, joking, laughing and enjoying a drink in their favourite pub. Now they were here. Shocked, panicked and desolate.

Poole had received a message from his mother's phone that simply read:

ONE DOWN, TWO TO GO...

They had rushed straight back to his apartment, but she had gone. Her purse and handbag were still there, and there were no signs of a struggle. He had no idea what was going to happen next; no idea when or even if they would see Jenny Poole again. All Brock knew was that he had to be there for Poole.

"Come on," Brock said placing one hand on Poole's shoulder. "Come back to ours tonight, there's nothing else we can do here now."

Poole snapped his head towards him, his face suddenly flashing with anger.

Brock prepared himself for a volley of angry words about how they couldn't just stop and go to bed, that they couldn't leave. Instead, though, the young sergeant's body sagged as his eyes, shining with emotion in the dim streetlight, shone. He nodded and turned towards the car with Brock in tow.

They drove in silence. Brock occasionally glanced at Poole, who was driving on autopilot. His eyes glazed as he stared through the windscreen as the streets of Bexford rolled beneath them.

Poole pulled into Brock and Laura's small driveway in front of their modest suburban house and turned off the engine.

"Are you sure it's ok for me to stay?" Poole said in a hollow voice.

"Don't be daft, of course it is," Brock grumbled as he heaved his large frame from the car. He leaned back in where Poole was still sitting, rigid. "We're going to find her."

Poole nodded. "I know."

Brock headed down the short path to the front door and was relieved to hear the car door open and close behind him. He opened the front door and waited for Poole to enter before closing the door on the chilled night air.

"Oh, Guy!" Laura said, rushing down the hall to him and embracing him. Sanita was next, appearing from the kitchen with a nervous-looking Davies behind her. She took Poole's hand delicately and led him through to the kitchen as Laura and Davies questioned Brock.

"How is he?" Laura asked in hushed tones as she stepped on tiptoes and kissed her husband on the cheek.

"Quiet," Brock rumbled. "Sheila didn't find anything obvious at the flat, but she's taken some prints."

"Wouldn't whoever did it have worn gloves?" Davies asked.

Brock sighed, "Yes, Davies."

He turned and hung his coat on its hook. If even Davies had thought of wearing gloves, he didn't hold out much hope that the kidnapper hadn't thought of it.

"Are you running the case, Sir?" Davies continued.

"We won't be allowed near it, it's too personal. The force doesn't like people getting involved in investigations that involve their own family and friends. Sharp will be running it with Anderson."

"Bloody hell," Davies said, glancing over his shoulder towards the kitchen. "Does he know that?"

"Yes, he threw the mug of tea we'd made him about forty foot down the street when I told him. That's when he went quiet. Come on, I need a drink."

The three of them headed into the kitchen where Poole and Sanita were sitting, her hands wrapped around his right hand as he stared at the table top.

He looked up at Brock as he entered.

"I'm going to make sure we find her, I don't care if it's official or not," Poole said looking him in the eye.

Brock nodded. "I wouldn't expect anything else, but it has to be off the books. In any case, the most important part of this might well be you and your father. We need to go over everything you know, everything that your mum has done or said recently. Anything could be relevant."

"This isn't about anything that happened recently," Poole said bitterly. "This is about what happened all those years ago. This is payback from the drug gang that my family got in the middle of."

Brock felt the tension in the room go up a notch.

On Poole's fifteenth birthday some members of a drug gang had driven past his house and fired indiscriminately into it from the moving vehicle. Poole had been shot in the leg and one of the two friends who had been sharing his big day with him had died. This terrible incident was the culmination of his parent's actions. His father, Jack Poole, for getting caught up in storing and moving drugs for the gang (whether knowingly or not was still up for debate in Brock's eyes), and his mother, Jenny Poole, for approaching the gang and asking them to leave Jack out of it, only to find she had approached the wrong gang and kicked off a gang war that arrived at their house soon after.

The connection between these past events and tonight was obvious. It had been the first thought of Brock and no doubt Poole. He knew though that they couldn't get too focused on this. It was all too easy to create your own narrative and fit facts to it rather than allow the facts to present their own conclusion.

"That seems the most likely explanation, but we have to treat this as any other case. Nothing gets ruled out, nothing gets ignored."

Poole nodded and wiped at his eyes.

"Not tonight though," Brock said. "Tonight the official investigation will be gathering everything they can. They've already spoken to both you and your father, there's no more to be done tonight."

Brock watched as Poole wrestled with this, but after a few moments, he nodded.

When they had spoken to Jack Poole earlier, he had been pale and quiet, a mirror image of his son's worry. He had given his statement to the police, patted his son on the shoulder and vanished off into the night with two heavies next to him, promising to put feelers out across his contacts for any news of who had done this, or why. They hadn't heard anything since.

Although Brock didn't want to focus solely on the incident that had changed his sergeant's life all those years ago, he had to admit that he agreed with Poole about the reasons his mother had been kidnapped. People weren't abducted from those on a modest salary such as Poole's, where any ransom would be paltry. These kinds of kidnappings were usually done for revenge and the message Poole had received, sent from Jenny Poole's own phone, seemed to make it clear that the family were being targeted. Jack, Jenny, and Guy Poole.

Brock had a sinking feeling that the chances of ever seeing Jenny Poole alive again were slim, but he was determined that her son wouldn't suffer the same fate.

CHAPTER TWO

"No one knows anything," Jack said as they gathered around the Brocks' kitchen table early on the third morning since Jenny Poole had vanished. "I've checked everywhere, asked everyone. Whoever did this didn't use anybody local."

"And what about back in London?" Poole asked, his voice tight and tense.

"None of the people who were involved..." he paused, his eyes darting towards his son, "back then," he continued, "are left. They're all either in prison, dead, or have gone legit with families of their own."

"It has to be someone from then," Poole said, his fists balling on the table.

Jack stared across the table at him. Brock could see the guilt from the shooting incident still etched on his face, as he guessed it always would be.

"Guy," Jack said softly. "You've got to remember that although it was a life-changing moment for us, it was just another day in the office for them. No one is still holding a grudge from back then."

"Well, I bloody am!" Guy shouted suddenly, slamming his fist down on the table in front of him and sending the various cups of coffee spilling onto the surface.

There was a tense silence as Laura and Brock exchanged glances before returning their gaze to the bowed head of Poole.

Poole's mother's disappearance had become a waiting game, one in which they were all powerless to help.

Poole had been staying with the Brock's since the disappearance. Brock told him it was so that they could discuss the case privately away from the station, but they both knew the real reason was for the safety of his sergeant.

"So what do we do next?" Guy said.

"We wait and see what they can uncover at the station," Brock said. They'd had this conversation before, but he knew this wouldn't be the last. "CCTV cameras around the area have all been checked, but there's nothing on them to give a clue and the coverage is patchy at best. It doesn't look like we have any forensics to go on, and Jenny's bank cards have all been left open, but no one's used them."

"So you're telling me that there's nothing we can do unless we hear from the kidnapper again?"

"We can keep thinking," Brock answered firmly. "Go over anyone who might have a grudge against either of you or your mum."

Poole turned to his father and spoke in a hard tone. "Something tells me the list of people wanting to hurt you is going to be longer than for me and mum."

"Maybe, maybe not," Jack said calmly. "I don't have a lot of enemies, people want to work with me, not against me."

"And what work is that exactly?" Poole snapped.

Jack paused for a moment. "Nothing that would relate to what's happened here," he answered in a low, steady voice.

Poole gave a mocking, exasperated chuckle and shook his head.

"I'm going to go," Jack said, standing up straight from where he had been leaning on the kitchen worktop. "I'll carry on putting the feelers out. Keep me up to date on what they find down at the station."

Poole said nothing, so Brock nodded and rose from his seat. "We will, Jack. The best chance of getting Jenny back is by working together as much as possible."

Jack nodded, and Brock followed him out into the hallway.

"I need you to look after him," Jack said, pausing with his hand on the front door handle. "You're the one he listens to."

"I will," Brock answered. "But if I find out there is anything you're not telling us about this," he paused, taking a deep breath. "Let's just say it might be best for you if you left Bexford."

"I'll stay where my son is," Jack replied curtly. "And I'd hold nothing back that could save Jenny's life."

He held Brock's gaze for a moment before turning and leaving through the front door, his eyes shining with emotion. So, Brock thought, Jack Poole did still care about his ex-wife.

Brock's phone buzzed in his pocket.

"Hello?"

"Sir? It's Davies, I'm at the station."

"What's the latest?" Brock barked, eager for anything that could provide a chink of light.

"Nothing much on Jenny, Sir. They've been interviewing her friends, but nobody seems to have a clue. They've found her phone at last, but it'd been smashed and dumped in a bin near the centre of town. Probably ditched it right after the text to Sergeant Poole."

"And no word from the kidnappers?"

"Nothing, Sir, they've set up monitoring on Sergeant Poole's phone though, so if they call they can try to find out where from."

Brock sighed. As a confirmed technophobe, he had no idea how any of this worked and he suspected Davies was none the wiser either, but he knew services had been called in from London and the phone companies had been contacted. He also knew that a missing woman in Bexford and one threatening text message wouldn't be seen as the highest priority over there. Not until there was more concrete evidence that she had actually been taken against her will. One message from her own phone wouldn't do that. In fact, it hadn't been enough to convince everyone at Bexford.

"Ok, Davies, keep us informed. We'll be in later."

"Actually, Sir, that's not why I was calling. There's a case."

"You've got to be bloody joking?"

"No, Sir. Sorry, Sir. Chief Inspector Tannock wants you to take it, Sir. It's a murder."

"Bloody hell," Brock muttered. "Ok, let me sort things out here and then I'll come into the station. Send me the details, will you?"

He hung up and headed back into the kitchen in a thunderous mood.

"What's happened?!" Laura said, seeing his expression.

Poole looked up at him, fear etched across his face.

"There's no news on Jenny," he said quickly, wanting to placate them. "They found her phone dumped in town, they're interviewing people who knew her."

"Let's get to the station," Poole said. "At least I'll feel as though I'm there if anything happens."

Brock nodded. "I think that's best, you'll be safe there as well. I might need to get you to drop me somewhere on the way through, I've got a case."

"A case?" Poole said, as though the idea that the world was continuing regardless had come as a surprise to him. "What is it?"

"A murder, Davies is sending me the details."

"Right," Poole said, standing. "Thank you again for having me, Laura." he said, turning to her.

"Don't be silly, you're welcome as long as you want." She rose and hugged him before he headed down the hall.

"Look after him, won't you?" Laura placing her head on Brock's wide chest.

"I will." Brock exhaled slowly, wishing people

would stop asking him that. He pulled back and looked at her, a hand on each shoulder. "Are you ok?"

"I'm fine, you don't need to worry about me as well."

Brock kissed her. "I'll always worry about you," he said, placing his hand on her stomach where their unborn child grew. They both smiled.

As he made his way out to the car where Poole had started the engine, his mind turned with just one of the many things that had worried him about the last few days. With Poole being a target and staying at his house, he could be putting both Laura and their child at risk.

CHAPTER THREE

Poole paused as they reached the steps of the station, turning away back towards the car park they had just walked from and exhaling slowly.

"You ok, Poole?" Brock asked, knowing it was a stupid question. He hadn't been to the station since his mother had disappeared. Brock hadn't let him, fearful of how he would react to the investigation going on in such close proximity. Today his temporary ban had not been mentioned. Brock reasoned that spending too long waiting around at his house would also send him stir-crazy. In any case, the less time they spent at home, the safer Laura might be.

"Fine," Poole answered after a few moments, he took another deep breath and turned back towards the door and heading up the steps.

"Oh, hello, Sir," Roland Hale said to Poole from behind the desk in reception. He had paused with a half-eaten sausage roll en route to his lips, ketchup already smeared down his left cheek. "We didn't expect to see you here today."

Brock shot him a look that suggested if there were any of his usual sarcastic humour, he would likely be removing a size fourteen boot from his rear end for the rest of the day.

Instead, he took another large bite of the sausage roll as he watched them swipe through the security door and into the main station.

Brock could feel the change in atmosphere as soon as they had entered. The people stationed at the numerous desks which covered the large room were doing their best not to stare, but their eyes twitched towards them constantly and the soft sound of whispered conversations drifted around the white walls.

"We'll go straight to Sharp's office and see if there's any news," Brock said, wanting to get Poole away from this atmosphere of intrigue, gossip and, worst of all, pity.

They walked straight through the line of desks, noticing that both Constable Sanita Sanders and David Davies were not at their shared desk. For the time being, it felt as though friends were scarce.

They stepped out of the main office and into a corridor where Brock rapped on the door that bore Detective Inspector Roderick Sharp's name in the form of a cheap plaque.

"Come in," barked the familiar, clipped tones of Sharp.

Brock was opening the door before the words had even finished. He stepped into the room, taking care to leave enough of his considerable bulk in the doorway to prevent Poole from entering the room fully.

"What's the latest, Sharp?"

"Now, come on Sam," the squat figure bristled behind the cheap desk. "I know your young Sergeant here is worried, but we have to play this by the book. I can't discuss an active case."

Brock took a long, slow breath as he looked around the small room.

Sergeant Anderson's chair squeaked as he shifted his weight under the intense stare. He was sitting at a smaller desk in the corner, the layout a mirror image of Brock and Poole's desk across the hall.

"In any case," Sharp continued, wilting under the silent tension. "There's not much to report, you know how it is in these cases. No sign of a struggle, victim texts some cryptic message from their own phone and from all accounts the woman's the type to run off at a moment's notice in any case."

Brock felt Poole tense next to him and watched as Anderson's lip curled into a sneer.

"Wait outside, Poole," he said in a quiet rumble.

Poole didn't move.

"That's an order, Sergeant."

Poole relented and turned back into the corridor.

Brock shuffled further over in the small space and closed the door behind him.

"You're going to continue to investigate this," he rumbled, "you're going to investigate this as though it was a member of your own family that had been kidnapped, and do you know why? Because it is. Whether you and your blonde meathead over here choose to accept it or not, that's what we are here. We have to work as one, it's what gives us the edge over the bad guys out there. You'll investigate this, and you'll keep me informed of everything you find out, ok?"

There was a moment of silence before Sharp unnecessarily cleared his throat and began arranging pens into a line on his desk.

"Well, of course. No stone unturned and all that. Wouldn't dream of not taking it seriously."

"Who have you spoken to already?" Brock asked, turning to Anderson.

"Some woman called Angela who's Jenny Poole's friend, apparently. Hasn't seen her or heard from her," he shrugged. "And some chap called Ricardo who didn't know anything either, but seems to have been her lover."

Brock watched the smirk and resisted the urge to flatten the blonde man's Roman nose across his face.

Instead, he leaned over until his face was inches from the young man's.

"I don't think you want to disappoint me on this one, Anderson. No matter what beef you have with Poole, it will pale into insignificance compared to the absolute world of fury you'll discover if Jenny Poole dies because you weren't doing your job properly." He wrenched the door open, stormed into the hall and slammed it behind him.

Poole was standing, leaning against the corridor of the wall, an intense look on his face.

"You're coming on this case with me," Brock said, walking past him without making eye contact.

"No," Poole said softly. "I need to stay here."

Brock stopped and turned slowly.

"Listen to me, Poole, if you stay here you're going to end up killing one of those two in there, and if you do that, you're losing the only two idiots who can actually do anything officially. Come with me and we'll look into this new case while we wait for news about your mum, and we'll run our own little investigation alongside."

"Is this an order, Sir?" Poole asked, standing up straight.

"Actually, Poole," Brock said, hitching up his trousers. "I think this time you're going to have to make your own mind up, but maybe take it as advice from a friend."

They held each other's gaze for a moment before Poole took a deep breath and nodded.

"Then we'd better go," Brock said, slapping Poole on the shoulder and guiding him towards the exit.

CHAPTER FOUR

The twenty-minute car journey out from the town of Bexford and into the Addervale countryside had mostly been spent in silence. Poole drove steadily, and Brock gazed out of the window in thought until his sergeant broke the quiet.

"There's something that doesn't make sense about all this," he said, his eyes fixed on the narrow country road ahead of them.

"Go on," Brock said.

"Well, twice in the last week I thought someone was following me. If that person is the same person that's taken mum, then they've been tracking us, maybe for a while."

"Right," Brock agreed. Again, they had already been over this.

"Which points towards some kind of revenge hit for whatever happened ten years ago,"

Brock watched as a flash of pain passed across the young man's narrow face. Though the incident had been ten years ago, he knew that it was still as fresh in his mind as if it had been yesterday.

"Think about it though," Poole continued. "The kind of people who run in drug gangs capable of shooting up a family home doesn't seem the type to kidnap. I think they would have just killed her." He swallowed and licked his lips. "Maybe they have?"

"No," Brock said firmly. "There's no point in thinking like that."

"Hold on though," Poole said, as though he hadn't been listening. "If that's what they wanted to do, they would have killed me too. Think of the message they sent, that they had mum, and that there were two to go. That has to be me and dad. If they were following me and knew that mum was staying with me, they could have got to us both."

Brock frowned. "I see what you're saying. Why not just kill the both of you?"

"Exactly!" Poole said, slapping the steering wheel with a surprising amount of force. "Which means they must want something else from this."

"Money?" Brock asked, already knowing the answer.

Poole gave a humourless laugh. "Well, good luck to them if that's what they want. Mum and I don't have a penny."

"And your dad?"

"I... I don't know," he said, his voice trailing off. "But there's been no ransom demand."

"True. So, what are you thinking?"

"I don't know," Poole snapped. He stared out through the windscreen, his jaw set. "Here it is," he added as he turned the car right past a sign which read Sundown Farm Retreat.

Brock noticed Poole's knuckles were white as his hands gripped the wheel and felt a pang of guilt as he found himself hoping that the murder case they were heading to would prove a distraction.

CHAPTER FIVE

———————————

Brock didn't have much experience with farmyards. Meat, eggs and cereals were things that came from shops far as he was concerned. He was well aware that there was hard work and muck involved somewhere down the line before that stage, but it didn't interest him as long as it all arrived in his local shop and then eventually on his plate.

Despite his lack of knowledge in this area, this was not what he had expected a farmyard to look like.

"It's a bit... clean, isn't it?" He said as he wrestled himself out of the car with some difficulty before stepping onto the pea-gravel floor with a crunch. The farmyard was a very bare, wide circle leading to various outbuildings which looked as suspiciously clean as the yard. There was no grain, no hay, and the only thing to even vaguely resemble farming equipment was a golf buggy that was parked between two of the outbuildings.

"Something tells me this isn't a normal kind of farm," Poole agreed. "I guess the 'retreat' part of the name might have something to do with it," Poole said.

"You're not wrong there," came the light Yorkshire tones of Sanita Sanders.

They turned to see her emerging from the main farmhouse and jogging down the few steps down from its small, stone porch. "Guy," she said softly, turning to him. Her golden skin shone in the weak, early morning sun as her familiar, lopsided smile broke out and she embraced Poole.

Brock looked away, partly through embarrassment, and partly because he didn't want to have to rebuke the constable for not being professional at a crime scene. He knew that due to Sanita's shifts, they had barely seen each other since Jenny had gone missing.

He cleared his throat loudly.

"So Constable Sanders, what have we got?"

He turned back as she pulled away from his sergeant, whose eyes blinked hazily.

"A murder, Sir. One of the owners of the place here."

"Is Sheila here?"

"Yes, Sir," Sanders replied.

Brock nodded, happy that the crime scene team, led by Sheila, were on the case already.

"And Ron's on his way," Sanders added, slightly cautiously.

"Right," Brock grunted through gritted teeth. He was not quite as happy at the imminent arrival of the local coroner. "Come on, Poole, let's go and take a look, shall we? Lead the way, Constable."

Sanders led them into the main farmhouse which, like the other buildings, had been scrubbed of every last trace of a working farm.

Inside was a hallway lit by bright spotlights that reflected off the hardwood floor. A long table to the left was filled with leaflets that Brock noticed ranged from yoga to massage, and even a session for something called fine-tuning for the soul.

"So what is this place?" he asked as Sanders led them through a door on the right. The door opened out into a large room, at the far end of which was a small group of people sitting on beanbags and looking thoroughly miserable.

"It's a retreat for business people to come away, bond and relax. They do yoga and things," she said, shrugging.

The people gathered at the far end of the room

had looked up as they entered, but had stayed seated. Only one woman had moved towards them. She had been standing, unlike the others, and they watched as she barged past the gangly figure of Constable Davies who had clearly been left to look after the witnesses and headed straight for them.

"Are you the Inspector?" she said in a curt manner. She was a short and somewhat stocky woman of middle-age who wore her brown hair in a bun. Her two-piece tweed suit gave her the air of a businessman woman, but one born of country life. She looked as though she would have been equally at home with either running through the last month's cash flow or out in the fields shooting wild game.

"I'm Detective Inspector Brock and this is Detective Sergeant Poole," Brock said. "And you are?"

"I am Nora Russell, I own this place, and I am also the general manager. I want to know why you are keeping my guests here like caged rats!"

"The owner?" Brock said, one eyebrow rising. He turned to Sanders.

"It was her partner that was killed, Sir," she said by way of explanation.

Brock nodded and turned back to the woman who had folded her arms and was now tapping her foot on the wooden floor.

"These guests of yours, what are they here for exactly?"

"We are a centre for relaxation and spiritual alignment. Businesses come to us to help their staff to grow as people and become more effective workers as a result."

"Right," Brock said slowly. He wasn't sure he had understood it completely, but he got the gist of it. They took suckers from the city, burned some incense in front of them and told them they'd had a spiritual awakening. Lord knows how much they charged per night, but he bet it would make his eyes water.

"And your guests at the moment are from a single company?" he continued.

"That's right, Comet Design. They're a web development company."

More words that were mostly meaningless to Brock.

"And they are just that, guests. I'm sure you can see how unreasonable it is that they are held here after this unpleasantness," she said pointedly.

"You would prefer we just sent them all home now, rather than check if any of them murdered your partner first?" Brock said with a raised eyebrow.

Nora Russell scowled and opened her mouth when Poole interjected before she could speak.

"I assure you that we will be releasing people as soon as we have managed to establish the facts around your partner's death," Poole said smoothly. "If you would just please take a seat with the others."

The woman gave a snort of derision but turned and headed back all the same.

"Well done, Poole," Brock said. "I was about to have one of my undiplomatic spells. Where's the crime scene?" he asked, looking around.

"It's in here, Sir," Sanders said, pointing to a box room that had been built into the corner of the larger, barn-like room. Its door lay open and through it, they could see the white-suited figure of Sheila Hopkins, Bexford's crime scene manager.

"Morning, Sheila," Brock said as they approached.

Sheila turned towards them from the assistant to whom she had been talking. "Oh, good morning, Sam." Her eye drifted to Poole's. "What are you doing here, Guy? Shouldn't you be at home?"

"I'm fine," Poole answered, a little more forcefully than was necessary.

Sheila nodded and turned to the body that was sitting upright in a large brown leather chair behind the desk towards the back of the room. The desk was almost empty, with only a small set of wooden statues in one corner and a simple earthenware bowl. There was no sign that anyone actually worked at this desk at all.

Another desk lay to their right against the wall and was the complete opposite to its partner. On its right-hand side lay a stack of trays that contained various papers and a large silver Dictaphone, and a laptop to the left. A well-used notepad was positioned next to the phone at the back and notes were pinned across a noticeboard on the wall overlooking it.

"Man in his late forties," Sheila began, gesturing to the victim, "looks like he's been stabbed and there was a knife next to him on the ground which was covered in blood and also looks like it's covered in prints."

Brock moved round to the side of the desk and looked down at the body in front of him.

The man was laying back in the chair, his dead eyes gazing up at the ceiling. His hair was a mass of greying curls that reached his shoulder and a short beard covered his face. He looked lean and toned with tanned skin that suggested he spent a lot of time outdoors. He wore a loose, white linen robe that had a dark red circle of blood across his chest.

"He looks like the bloody Japanese flag," Brock

grumbled as he peered down at what he could see of the wound. "Why did you say 'it looks like he's been stabbed' rather than just saying that 'he's been stabbed'?" he asked Sheila.

She gave a confused smile as she looked down at the victim. "You'll need to ask Ron, not me, but it looks as though someone's not just stuck the knife in, they've jiggled it about a bit as well, the wound looks messy to me."

"You've got such a way with words," Brock grimaced. "So," he said, standing back from the body and looking around the space. "Where's the murder weapon?" Poole asked.

"I was hoping you'd ask that," she answered, smiling. She lifted up a large evidence bag with a long thin blade inside it. Brock took it from her and held it up to the light from the spotlights that studded the ceiling. The blade was almost a foot long. Its handle was carved wood, though through the bag it was hard to make out what the carvings were depicting. He handed it to Poole to inspect.

"What sort of knife is this?" the sergeant said before handing it back to Sheila.

"Well, I've never seen anything like it, but look at this." She shifted the bag around as she peered through its translucent surface. "Here you go," she said, pulling the plastic tight and turning it back to him.

He leaned in. "Are those breasts?"

"They are, and believe me it only gets ruder when you start seeing how all the figures fit together," Sheila said with a smirk. "In any case, it has a load of prints, I'm going to have to get it back to the lab before I can pull them all off correctly."

"Ok, well as soon as you're done here, if you don't mind."

"Of course," Sheila nodded. "And if you need anything Guy, you just have to call."

"Thank you, Sheila," Poole said with a forced smile. He turned to head out of the room and paused. "This door's been forced," he said, bending down to the lock.

"It has, they broke in when there wasn't any answer," Sheila replied.

"And who was it that found him then?" Brock asked.

"Well, according to Sanita, it was all of them at once," Sheila shrugged.

"And Ron is on his way?" Brock asked somewhat tentatively. He had a long-standing hatred of the coroner and preferred to have as little to do with him as his job would allow.

"No," Sheila replied, smiling. "He was away on

some course or other. He's cut it short, but he won't be back until tomorrow."

"Can I poke around a bit?" Brock asked. Sheila nodded and passed him and Poole a pair of latex gloves each.

They each pulled them on and began to run their experienced eyes over the office. Poole began looking through the bookshelves that ran along the left-hand wall, while Brock began glancing through the papers on the right-hand desk. There was nothing of immediate interest. Some bills, a few receipts for purchases of catering supplies and firewood.

He lifted up the Dictaphone and peered hopelessly at the buttons.

"I've already checked. Nothing on it," Sheila said from behind him.

He replaced it with relief. Being confronted with technology brought him out in cold sweats.

"We've looked over most things," Sheila continued, "Can't see anything obvious, nothing jumps out."

"Come on then, Poole," Brock said, pulling his gloves off, "shall we get talking to some of this ill-fated rescue party?"

"Yes, Sir," Poole replied, his voice distant, before stepping out of the room.

Brock followed him, concerned at his young colleague's quietness.

He wondered if he should, in fact, send him back to the station, or maybe even to his flat, but he knew it would be the wrong move. Nobody at the station was going to take this seriously until they had a ransom demand, and if he went home, he would just end up being a target himself.

"Are you ok being here, Poole?" Brock asked as they walked back to the group at the other end of the long hall.

"I don't think I've got much choice, Sir," he answered. "I can't do anything until whoever took mum makes a move. At least this is keeping my mind busy."

Brock nodded, though he wasn't sure he believed his young partner. He had barely said a word since they'd arrived and he doubted he was following the case. Importantly though, Brock could keep an eye on him here. He could look out for him.

"I've set up a room for interviews, Sir," Sanders said, coming across from the group towards them. "It's a meditation room, not very big, but it was pretty empty at least. I found three chairs and stuck them in there." She gave one of her lopsided grins. "I'm afraid Nora Russell is insisting she talks to you first."

"Ah, the toe-tapper!" Brock smiled. "By all

means, let's see what she has to say when she's not being impatient and stroppy, shall we?"

"I've only been here an hour," Sanders said, "but I'm not sure she has a setting that isn't impatient and stroppy, Sir."

CHAPTER SIX

N ora Russell was sitting before them with knees together, and her hands clasped together on top of them. She had a plain face that could have been quite pleasant if it hadn't been pinched into the scowl she seemed to wear at all times.

"I have already been through all this with the constable," she said primly.

"I am aware of that, but we need you to go over it one more time, if you don't mind," Brock said in what he hoped sounded like a pleasant tone.

He had never been good at putting people like Nora Russell at ease. Tightly wound busybodies like her needed to be coaxed into cooperation, which was something more in Poole's skill set than his own. But as his wife often said, there's no dog too old to learn new tricks. Though she tended to say this about his reluctance to embrace technology, and he was fairly sure that was a trick he would never be learning.

"I was waiting in the office for Moonlake to arrive and..."

"I'm sorry," Brock said, his hand raised before him. "Did you say Moonlake?"

"That's the name that Christopher had decided to be known by," she said, her tone making Brock think that she shared his opinion on this name choice. "He had told me that he needed to talk to me while the guests were in their morning relaxation period and so I went to the office and waited."

"And where were the guests having their morning relaxation period?" Poole asked.

"We let them rise when they want, but there are no curtains on the bedrooms here to encourage people to rise with the sun," she paused with her closed lips moving as though she was tasting something repugnant. "And they usually do. Then they gather in the open room, the one outside the office that you were in earlier. Moonlake," she paused, "Christopher came in and began ranting about the financial industry he used to work in. I had no idea what had set him off, but he was furious about whatever it was. In the end I left him shouting to himself and told the others to just wait until he was ready to begin. I came back an hour later, and they were all still sitting around so I went to the office to get him, but it was locked."

"Didn't you have a key?" Poole asked.

"I did, but it was hanging on my key hook in the office. Christopher and I shared the space."

Brock nodded. "We saw the two desks," he said. "So, what did you do when you found the door locked?"

"I called over to the others," she said, in a tone that suggested Brock should have known this. "I'm not exactly the door-breaking-down type. Glenn Weaver, one of the guests, broke it down."

"And you found Mr Lake as we saw him this morning?"

"Yes."

Brock watched her closely, remembering the sight of her dead partner didn't seem to have upset her as one might expect. Her face remained as hard and business-like as it had done throughout the interview.

"Were you and your partner close?"

Again, her lips writhed for a moment before speaking. "We had our differences, I won't lie, but Christopher was an important part of this place."

"The murder weapon, did you see it?"

"The knife? Of course, I could hardly have

missed it. It's the knife Christopher used in his ceremonies."

"What ceremonies?"

"You'd be better off talking to the guests about that, I didn't get involved in the more spiritual side of things, that was Christopher's domain. I handled the business."

"And was business going well?" Poole asked.

"Very well, thank you."

"And did Christopher have any family? Who inherits his share of the business?" Poole pressed.

"I know what you're getting at, Sergeant. Christopher didn't have any family, no. And yes, I do gain his share in the business, but I didn't kill him. It will be hard to run the retreat without its spiritual leader, don't you think?"

"Will you try to keep it going?"

"I haven't made plans as yet, we only found Christopher a few hours ago."

"Of course, I'm sorry for your loss."

She nodded, looking satisfied for the first time since they had met her.

"Thank you, that will be all for now." Brock said. He watched her leave and sank back a little into his chair, frowning. That hadn't been quite what he had expected. He had sensed, when they had first met the woman outside the office where her partner was murdered, that there was going to be a feistiness and anger about her. Instead, she had seemed controlled and unfeeling. He turned his gaze to Poole, who was also deep in thought. "So, what do you make of her, Poole?"

"I can't get a read on her. She seems so cold it's hard to tell what she's really thinking or feeling."

"I'm not sure she's feeling much," Brock replied, "but she's thinking of what to do next that's for sure. The only time I definitely thought I saw any emotion in her was when you asked her about her plans for the retreat. Somebody like Nora Russell doesn't stop making plans, ever."

CHAPTER SEVEN

G lenn Weaver was a good-looking young man with light brown hair and dark brown eyes that darted between Brock and Poole nervously as he shifted on his chair.

"Yes, I broke down the door. Someone had to." He shrugged.

"And when you got through the door? What happened next?"

"Next? What do you mean 'next'? Moonlake was bloody dead, wasn't he! With a knife sticking out of his chest!"

"And did anyone go to him?"

He shrugged again. "No point, everyone could see straight away that he was dead."

"And when had you last seen him before he died?"

"About twenty minutes before. He walked into the room and went straight in the office. We heard him and Nora having a blazing row and then she left, he carried on ranting for a bit and then it went quiet."

"And nobody else went in or out of the office?"

"Nope, we would have seen them, and none of us moved I can tell you that much."

"And do you know of anyone that might have wanted to hurt Christopher Lake?"

The young man frowned, his left hand reaching up and scratching at his square jaw that was covered in stubble. "There'd been a bit of friction over the last couple of days, but nothing anyone would have killed over."

"What sort of friction?" Poole asked.

"You should talk to Harold about that,"

Poole looked down at his notes. "Harold Olsen?"

"Yep, I saw him arguing with Moonlake yesterday."

"What were they arguing about?" Brock asked, leaning forward in his chair.

"I don't know, ask Harold!" the young man snapped. "Whatever it was, it was pretty heated. This place has been a disaster."

"What do you mean by that?"

He sighed and leaned back in his chair. The flash

of anger that had been there previously was now gone. Instead, he just looked tired.

"Matty brought us out here for some team-building, well-being nonsense and all it's done is make us put us all at each other's throats."

Brock raised an eyebrow and waited for the man to continue.

"Look, the place is nice enough, but Moonlake was an absolute loon! He had us doing all sorts of weird things. Look at the state of my arm!" He pulled back the right sleeve of his blue checked shirt to reveal a number of lines across the forearm.

"He cut you?!"

"No, we had to do it ourselves. Something about letting demons out of soul or some rubbish like that. As I said, the bloke was a loon and I think Matty realised because this morning she said we were all going home."

"When was this?"

"When we were all sitting in the open room waiting around for Moonlake to come out."

"And did no one think to go and knock on the door sooner?"

"Not the way he'd been ranting after Nora left. Anyway, no one was in the mood for more of his nonsense by then. We were taking the opportunity to relax without all of that crap."

"What can you tell me about the other people you work with?"

"Rosa is my fiancé," he said quickly. "The others are alright," he shrugged again.

"Congratulations," Poole said, looking down at his notes. "And you're a junior web designer, is that right?"

"I'm the one that does all the work if that's what you mean,"

"You feel you do more than your fair share?"

"These days Matty is always off talking to clients, which leaves me to sort things out by myself."

"And what does Rosa do?"

"Everything I don't," he said with a dry laugh. "She handles all the admin, deals with new clients and things as well."

"I think that's all for now," Brock said. "Could you send Rosa in next, please?"

"I do not like this at all, Poole," Brock said when Glenn had left. "If everyone sticks to the same story as the first two, we've got a whole room full of witnesses saying no one went in or out of that room the whole time they were sitting there."

"Which means we've got a locked room with only one entry and exit and somehow a man was murdered in it," Poole said.

They both leaned back in their chairs and

exhaled at the same time before Poole pulled his phone from his pocket.

Brock watched him as he glanced at the blank screen, took a deep breath and put it back in his pocket.

"No news?" Brock asked, already knowing the answer.

"Not that I was expecting any," Poole answered. "I think the next news I get will be the end of it all, anyway."

"Poole, You can't think like that, you need to..."

"I know, I know," the young sergeant said, holding one hand up as the door opened and Rosa Briggs stepped into the room.

CHAPTER EIGHT

R osa Briggs was a thin young woman with cheekbones so defined that they threatened to pierce through her skin. Her hair was a large mop of brown with blonde highlights and she wore an oversized jumper that hung off of one shoulder with skinny jeans.

"We understand that you are engaged to Glenn Weaver?" Brock asked once they had gone through the formalities of introduction.

The pale skin of her forehead furrowed. "I am," she said slowly.

Brock raised an eyebrow, but she didn't expand on the point. Instead, she crossed her denim-clad legs and eyed the two of them.

"It's pretty obvious that Moonlake killed himself," she said in a matter-of-fact tone.

"What makes you say that? Did Mr Lake seem down or depressed at all this week?"

"Lord, no!" She laughed, her head tilting backwards. Then, in a suddenly darker, more bitter tone, "He was always happy as anything," she looked up at them, the lightness returning to her voice. "That's the way it is though sometimes, isn't it? People who are happy all the time are always masking something, right?"

"And what do you think Mr Lake was masking?"

"I wouldn't have a clue, but it's obvious he must have done it himself. We were all sitting right there, there's no way anyone could have got in or out without us seeing."

"And no one got up to go to the toilet at any time?"

"No, we were only there just over an hour or so."

Brock nodded thoughtfully. "Ok, Miss Briggs, can you send in Harold Olsen please?"

The young woman got up and left, leaving them alone again.

"You're leaving the company owner until last," Poole said, "can I ask why?"

"Because I'm hoping that she's the one to give us the proper story on all the others, she hired them after all. I wanted to meet them first though, make my own impressions, then I can compare with what she comes up with."

"Makes sense," Poole said as the door opened again.

Harold Olsen was a small, balding man who looked as though he had just crawled out from underground. He blinked at them from behind round, thick-lensed glasses and took his seat neatly, hands resting on the table between them.

"Mr Olsen, I believe you handle the finances at Comet Design?"

"That's right,"

"And were you enjoying your stay here at the retreat?"

"To tell you the truth, no, I wasn't. The whole thing was a silly load of nonsense."

"And what did you think of Mr Lake?"

The little man swallowed. "I'm sorry about what happened to him obviously, but I can't say I knew him well enough to form an opinion."

"Other than to say that the things he believed in and practised here were a load of silly nonsense?" Poole said.

Brock smiled automatically, and then quickly wiped it from his face. Poole was getting the hang of this, he was even beginning to sound like him.

"Well, I can't say I agreed with all this," he said,

waving his arms at the masks and dreamcatchers which lined the walls. "But I wouldn't want to comment on the man."

"We heard that you had an argument with Mr Lake yesterday," Brock said, watching him carefully.

The man blinked furiously. "I merely had a small disagreement with him, it was nothing."

"Can you tell me what it was about?"

Harold licked his lips as he removed his glasses and cleaned them on his grey cardigan. "I didn't like the way he had been treating some of the other members of the team," he said quietly before replacing his glasses.

"In what way?"

"Let's just say he paid a little more attention to our female staff than I thought was appropriate."

"You mean he was coming on to them?" Poole asked.

"I'm not going to say anything more on the subject, you can ask them if you really have to."

They ran through the events of the morning and the discovery of the body, but his story was the same as everyone else's. No one had entered the office during the time they had been outside it. They let Olsen leave, and a few moments later they were joined by Matilda Heck.

She had wide, dark eyes which flashed under

long false eyelashes. She had a mass of dark hair which framed her narrow face with its bright white smile.

"Inspector, obviously this is a tragedy," she said as she swept into the room, her large hoop earrings swinging as she made her way across the room to the chair in front of them. "Everyone from Comet Design will cooperate fully of course, but I must say that I would rather we could all get out of here as soon as possible."

"And why would that be, Mrs Heck?" Brock asked.

She leaned across the table and put her hand on his. "It's Miss Heck, actually," she said, smiling, "But you can call me Matty."

Brock pulled his hand away quickly and placed it on his lap under the table. "Can you just answer the question please, Miss Heck?" He said gruffly.

"Well, we hardly want to hang around here, do we?!" She laughed. "Not with poor Moonlake topping himself."

"Can you tell me why you brought your firm here?"

"Because I was a sucker," she laughed. "We were taken on to design the website for the retreat and when we'd already sunk a decent amount of hours into it they said they were having difficulty covering the bill, so they offered some time here as part payment. Like an idiot, I agreed to take it."

"So you haven't been overly happy with your stay here?" Poole asked.

"You mean before the spiritual guru we were supposed to be learning from killed himself?" she said, dripping with sarcasm. "No, not particularly. I'm afraid I saw through the setup here rather quickly."

"What do you mean saw through it?"

"Well, Moonlake is... was, no more a spiritual guru than I am. He was a chancer who had stumbled on an act that he used to convince other people to listen to him. Which, I think, when it came down to it, was all he ever wanted."

"Can you tell us a bit about the people who work for you?" Poole asked.

"They're a decent bunch. I'm sure Glenn and Rosa have probably already told you that they do all the work?" She laughed as Brock nodded. "Well, they're not wrong, but then I stumped up the money to get the thing going, so I guess it's my prerogative to just be the public face of things these days. We do have several other designers, but they're all remote workers, the core of the team is all here. I thought it might be good for us." She shook her head as though this was, in hindsight, ridiculous.

"And did Mr Lake make any amorous advances towards you or the other members of your staff?" Brock asked.

"Amorous advances? My word, Inspector, you really are something out of a Jane Austen novel aren't you?" She smiled, her eyes sparkling mischievously. "Moonlake was very into freely expressing his emotions," she said carefully.

There was a knock on the door as it opened to reveal Constable Sanders peering through.

"Um, sorry, sirs, but I think you need to see this." She looked nervously at Poole, and Brock felt the hairs on the back of his neck stand up. Something had happened. Something to do with Jenny Poole.

CHAPTER NINE

Matilda Heck was ushered from the room and Sanders took the seat she had vacated.

"Look at this," she said, laying a large black appointment book in front of them and turning it around. Her finger ran down the page until she pointed at a name, written in blue ink.

Jenny Poole

"This is the appointment book for the retreat, apparently your mum was going to come here today," Sanders said, her hand reaching out to Poole's. He pulled away and got up, his chair scraping backwards on the wooden floor.

"We need to talk to Nora Russell right now, this second," he said, moving towards the door.

"Wait, Poole," Brock said.

His voice was quiet, but hard enough that Poole stopped in his tracks.

"We need to do this the right way. We'll call her back in here, take another statement from her."

Poole held his eye for a moment before nodding and taking his seat again.

"Give us a minute, and then send her in, Constable Sanders," Brock said.

She nodded, gave a worried glance at Poole and then left the room.

"I take it you didn't know anything about your mother coming here?" Brock asked.

"No, and I don't know why she would. The retreat is for businesses to come and team building, not for individuals. Although," he said with a humourless smile, "this place is definitely her kettle of fish."

"This is something though, Poole," Brock said. "Something we didn't have before, which is good news."

Poole nodded and leaned forward, his elbows on the desk.

Brock knew he was going to have to be careful here. This might mean nothing, but Jenny Poole having an appointment at a retreat where a man was murdered just before she went missing seemed too much of a coincidence.

"You wanted to see me again?" Nora Russell said as she opened the door.

"Yes, Miss Russell," Brock said, taking the lead.

She took a seat in the chair in front of them, her eyes glancing down at the appointment book in front of her.

"What's this doing here?" She frowned.

"This name," Brock said, pointing, "Jenny Poole. Why was she due to visit the retreat?"

Nora gave a snort of derision. "Christopher always had a constant flow of people willing to take his money in exchange for some ridiculous healing process." Brock felt Poole stiffen next to him.

"This woman," Nora continued, "knew something about crystals, I think, Christopher wanted to talk to her about kitting out the retreat. Make the energy of the building more positive or some nonsense."

"Did you make the appointment?" Brock asked.

"No, Christopher did. He was surprisingly happy to take on the business side of things when it suited him," she said bitterly.

"According to this, she was due here at two o'clock today?"

"I assume she still is," Nora shrugged. "What has this got to do with Christopher's death? Do you think this woman had something to do with it?"

"No," Poole said. "This woman went missing two days ago."

"Oh, well she hasn't been here I can tell you that, but I'm fairly sure Christopher made the appointment yesterday morning. I heard him talking about crystals on the office phone."

Poole turned to Brock, the significance of this not lost on either of them.

"Ok, Miss Russell, if you can remember anything else please let us know," Brock said, dismissing her from the room.

"It's too much of a coincidence, Sir," Poole said. "We need to tell Anderson and Sharp."

A flicker of a smile played on Brock's lips. Even in a situation like this Poole was trying to do the right thing, report the new information to the officers in charge of the case.

"I'll be blunt with you, Poole, Sharp and Anderson aren't going to look into this seriously until something happens, and this won't count in their eyes. If anything, it will just lead them to the conclusion that Jenny was free to make arrangements to talk about crystals after her phone sent you that message. No, I think we look into this ourselves. We're at the scene of a murder, and now your mother's name pops up. Something tells me that if we find out what happened to Christopher

Lake, it might shed light on what's happened to Jenny."

Poole looked down, thinking.

"It's all we have, Guy," Brock said softly.

Poole nodded, looking up with his eyes shining. "We need to look at the phone records for the phone in the office here," he said. "I want to see what number my mum apparently spoke to Lake on. We know it wasn't from her mobile, because we've got the records from her phone company."

Brock nodded. "We need to find out if there was any other connection between your mum and this Christopher Lake chap, and we need to find out which one of these people killed him."

"You think it was definitely someone here and not someone from outside, a robbery gone wrong maybe?" Poole asked.

"According to Nora Russell's initial statement, nothing has gone missing. In any case, I don't see how else it could have been done. Either way, someone had to get into that room to kill Christopher Lake, so one, or more, of the people here must know what happened. They've all told us that no one could have got past them without them noticing..."

"Which means someone's lying," Poole said, finishing his sentence.

"Exactly," Brock said grimly, "unless they all are,

of course. There's something about this that doesn't feel right Poole. How often is it that we get so many witnesses all agreeing on exactly what happened, and then them all agreeing that the murder was impossible?"

Poole looked thoughtful at this for a moment before looking up. "Unless Christopher Lake really did kill himself?"

"No one kills themselves by a knife to the chest. It takes force, for one thing. Someone has to plunge the thing in. That's hard to do to yourself, and there are definitely less painful ways to do it. There's something else that's bothering me as well, though."

"What's that, Sir?"

"This argument the victim had with Nora Russell. Everyone heard them going at each other, and then after Nora left they heard Lake still ranting away in his office, and then it went quiet."

"That's right."

"But none of them heard Lake shout at his attacker. He was stabbed in the chest, front and centre. He would have been looking his killer right in the eye. He'd already been ranting and raving and was clearly worked up, so why wasn't he shouting at his killer? Why didn't he put up a fight? There were no defensive wounds on his hands, I looked. It's almost as though the whole thing took him by surprise while he was sitting in his chair, but how on earth can that have happened? That office is so small, you'd see anyone else in it in a second." He looked up, realising that he was verbalising thoughts that he usually would keep close to his chest at this stage of an investigation, and saw that Poole was listening intently.

At least they had a new lead in the disappearance of Jenny Poole, but even that was clouded by fresh worries. He didn't want to tell Poole, but if the murder of Christopher Lake was tied to his mother's abduction, then things did not look good for her.

"Come on Poole, let's go and see what connections we can find between your mother and this place. I want to get out of here before Ron gets here in any case."

CHAPTER TEN

"Any news?!" cried Sal Bonetti as she burst out from behind the counter as soon as the small bell had rung above the door of Sal's sandwich shop. She embraced Poole, who was standing rather stiffly as her long, light brown arms embraced him. She wore a denim shirt over a white vest top and her large, dark eyes were filled with concern.

"We might have a lead," Poole said. "I don't suppose mum ever mentioned a place to you called Sundown Farm Retreat?"

"Not that I can remember," Sal said, her face screwed up as she searched her memory. "But I really haven't spoken to your mother very much, Guy. She often comes in with Ricardo, have you spoken to him?"

"He's coming here in a minute," Poole answered with gritted teeth.

"Make us something nice, will you, Sal?" Brock said. "We've had a bit of a morning."

"I always make you something nice!" she said sternly, before heading off back behind the counter.

They moved across to their usual table, Brock lowering himself slowly, always concerned that the narrow metal legs wouldn't hold his considerable bulk.

He looked across at his partner, who was staring out of the window into the street with a glazed expression. When he first met him he'd had the impression, the young man was made out of golf clubs. Tall, with long, wiry limbs and a sense of what was right that could take a blow from an iron bar and not be shaken. How had this man's life been so tainted by pain and trauma? How had he still been able to become the man he was when he could have so easily taken another path? One of bitterness and anger that could have twisted mind and soul.

"So what do you actually know about this Ricardo guy?" Brock asked.

"Not a lot, really. I thought at first that he was some chancer trying to take advantage of Mum, but he seems to have stuck around. Long enough to know that she hasn't got enough money to be worth a con job in any case."

"And he teaches yoga?"

"Apparently, and other things like that. He might know of this retreat even if he doesn't know anything about mum going there."

"Hopefully we'll get the phone records from the retreat soon." Brock too turned to look out of the window. "I'm glad we've persuaded the guests and Nora Russell to all stay there for now. That lot are a bit of a puzzle and we won't get to the bottom of Lake's murder if half of them jet off back to London."

They both looked up as the little bell above the cafe door rang once more and Ricardo Jevez entered.

Brock had only met the man once, and that had been briefly, bumping into Jenny and Ricardo in Bexford's town square one morning when searching for a rare breakfast out with his wife Laura. Looking at him again now, with a more professional eye, he was struck by how large and toned the man appeared. He wore a tight fitting t-shirt which accentuated his muscular body. He wasn't the bulky build of a weight lifter though, his was the lithe power that you got from eating well, exercising regularly and generally, in Brock's mind, not enjoying life.

"Guy," Ricardo said in a thick Colombian accent.

"How are you doing?" He took a seat between the two of them and peered at Poole, his head turning on one side.

"I'm ok," Poole said warily. He glanced across at Brock. "This is Inspector Brock," he said, nodding towards him.

Ricardo turned and extended a hand. "I am pleased to meet you, though I wish it was in better ways."

Brock nodded, noting that his English, although excellent, had its eccentricities. "I'm sorry, but we need to ask you a few further questions about Jenny."

"Of course, anything," Ricardo said before his head jerked back and he looked between them. "Have you found something out? Do you know where she is?!"

"No," Brock said quickly, "I'm afraid we don't. Something has come to light, though. Have you ever heard of the Sundown Farm Retreat?"

"Yes, of course." Ricardo frowned. "Why?"

"Can I ask how you know of the place?"

"I have worked there before," he answered bluntly. "Moonlake has called me in occasionally to take yoga classes for some of his clients."

"And did mum ever go there with you?" Poole asked.

"No," Ricardo answered, a puzzled look on his face. "What is this about?"

"I'm sorry to say that Christopher Lake was found dead this morning," Brock said.

"What?! How?!"

"He was stabbed in the chest."

Ricardo muttered a rush of prayers under his breath as he looked up to the heavens before looking back to them.

"You think this is something to do with Jenny going missing?"

"She was due to visit Christopher today," Poole said.

"What for?"

"We were hoping you could tell us that."

Ricardo paused, his deep brown eyes took on a questioning look.

"There was something a couple of weeks ago," he said slowly. "Jenny said that she had met someone who was interested in her crystals, maybe it was something to do with that?

"Did you ask her who was interested in her crystals?"

"Of course, but she said it was a surprise, which now I think about it, was strange."

"Why?" Poole asked.

"Because she would have told me." He shrugged.

"We tell each other everything." He lifted his chiselled chin and looked at Poole. "Your mother has a beautiful soul, Guy, and she is a strong woman. I know she will be ok."

Brock watched his partner's blank stare for a moment and decided to interject.

"I think that's it, thank you. If you think of anything else, please let us know immediately." He slid a business card across the table to him.

Ricardo picked it up and peered at it before standing.

"And you do the same for me, any news and I would like to know," he said.

"Of course," Poole said firmly, standing and shaking the man by the hand.

They watched him leave as Sal wandered over with two steaming plates of food.

"Here we go, we have two slices of sourdough toast with soft, sliced Italian sausage and sliced mushrooms cooked with crème fraîche, some parsley, butter and topped with a slice of prosciutto."

Brock's mouth was watering before the smell even hit his nose.

"Thank you, Sal," he said, as he took up his knife and fork.

"He's a good looking man, your friend Ricardo,"

she said with a twinkle in her eyes, before sashaying off back behind the counter.

Brock had wondered before what Sal's personal situation was but had never asked. He knew she had a son who lived in London, but he had no knowledge of a partner. With cooking as good and as devilish as hers, any partner she might have had before might well have eaten himself into an early grave, he thought as he tucked into the delicious dish in front of him.

"It sounds to me," he said between mouthfuls, "that Jenny was definitely planning on meeting Christopher Lake. The sooner we find answers at the retreat, the sooner we'll have something that will help us get her back."

Poole nodded but said nothing as he ate.

Brock was worried. The change in his young colleague's manner was startling. He was quiet and sullen now, which was to be expected, but there was something more troubling there. Brock felt as though his friend was hardening, that he was putting up barriers. Barriers that aren't so easily torn down.

CHAPTER ELEVEN

"Well, it looks like Nora Russell and Christopher Lake had a pretty standard partnership agreement," Poole said as he peered at his computer screen.

"Does it say anything about what would happen if one of them dies?" Brock asked from behind his desk.

"Yes, it says the other partner has the right to buy out the deceased partner, well, their family at any rate."

"So, Nora gets the chance to get her hands on the whole thing," Brock mused as he leaned back in his chair. "And there's still no word on next of kin for Lake?"

"No, nothing. His parents both died a number of

years ago and it looks like he never married or had children."

"What do we know about him? What was he up to before he got involved with the retreat?"

Poole pushed his chair back from his desk and turned towards Brock.

Their office was small, with one large desk in front of the back wall facing out, and Poole's smaller desk against the right-hand wall. The shelves on the left-hand wall were full of stuffed folders and piles of papers from various cases and enquiries. Brock was very much an offline man in an online world and always preferred his paperwork to be on paper. In fact, he mostly preferred for Poole to do it.

His sergeant opened a manila folder and scanned the sheets of paper inside.

"He was a finance guy in the city, worked for one of the big institutions before the banking crisis,"

"When he got laid off, I presume?"

"He did, but with a hefty pay-out. Then it looks as though he travelled a lot, spent quite a bit of time in India and then came back to the UK to set up the retreat."

"How long from when he lost his job to when he set up the place?"

"A little over a year, why?"

Brock smiled. "I was just wondering how long it takes to go from financial shark to meditating guru."

He watched the smile spread on Poole's face only for it to be instantly shut down as the young man frowned and looked back at the folder. Brock felt a pang of pity for his partner, seeing him in a brief moment where his thoughts weren't full of his mother's disappearance and he had smiled, before the nagging reality at the back of his mind had jerked him back again.

"So do we think it's unlikely that Christopher Lake and Jenny ever crossed paths before this meeting about crystals?" Brock said, hoping to keep them both focussed on the case in front of them.

"We do," Poole nodded. "I can't see how they would have met before."

Poole's phone buzzed loudly on his desk and he took it quickly and unlocked it, before staring intently at the message on the screen. "It's Dad," he said, sagging slightly at with the disappointment of it not being his mother. "He says he's still got nothing on Mum."

"It might be worth asking him to put the feelers out on the retreat, see if there's any dirt he can find on the place."

Poole nodded and began tapping onto the screen when there was a knock on the door.

"Come in," Brock said loudly.

The door opened and Detective Inspector Roderick Sharp stepped in. He paused as he saw Poole at his desk, before clearing his throat loudly and moving past the sergeant to Brock's desk.

"Saw you were back in the station, thought I'd come over," he said in a clipped tone. He glanced over his shoulder at Poole, who was staring daggers at him, before leaning forward and lowering his voice. "I wondered if I could have a word in private?"

"If this is about my mother, then you can tell me now," Poole said, rising for his chair so suddenly that Sharp stumbled backwards.

"No, no news on that front, just want a word with Brock here,"

There was a moment of strained silence before Brock spoke.

"Why don't you go and get us a couple of coffees, Poole, while I have a quick word with Sharp here."

Poole took a deep breath, then turned suddenly and left the room.

"He's upset," Sharp said as though just realising for the first time. "Perfectly natural, perfectly natural." He nodded, still staring at the door Poole had left through.

"What is it, Sharp?" Brock growled.

"Right, yes, of course," Sharp blustered before

clearing his throat unnecessarily loudly. "Just wanted to say that we will do our best for the boy's mother, if she has been taken, then I'll leave no stone unturned, but I think we've exhausted any reasonable avenues we could pursue." Brock watched him squirm for a moment before Sharp's reserved manner wilted under his gaze.

"For heaven's sake, Brock, there's nothing to go on!" he said imploringly, his arms spread wide, palms upwards. "I mean to say, what would you have me do, man?! There's no sign of the woman and no one seems to know anything about what's happened to her!"

"There's still no activity on her bank accounts?" Brock asked.

"Nothing,"

"And you've looked into her past? The shooting that took place at their family home ten years ago?"

"Yes, yes," Sharp said dismissively, regaining some of his usual pomposity. "There's nothing doing there. All the gangs that were involved have either vanished or turned into something else, but either way, no one is around to even remember what happened that day, let alone be still out looking for revenge or whatever."

Brock closed his eyes and exhaled through his broad nose. He had been afraid of this answer. If

Jenny Poole's disappearance wasn't linked to the shooting that had torn her family apart and seen her son wounded and his friend killed, then he held little hope of knowing what had happened to her. A simple kidnapping for ransom would have meant some form of contact by now, surely? Instead, there had been nothing. No phone calls, no activity on her bank accounts, not even a reported sighting. She had simply vanished, and that had left an icy ball of worry in his gut that spelled bad news.

"Don't give up on her Sharp. Poole's been through enough."

"Yes, well, do one's duty and all that," Sharp blustered before turning and heading out of the room, leaving Brock with a cold sense of helplessness.

CHAPTER TWELVE

The tall grass that filled fields either side of the driveway to the Sundown Farm Retreat rippled in the wind like gentle waves on a lake. The sun, too, was dappling the grass as quick-moving clouds above threw shadows across the field causing shafts of light to appear and vanish across the fields.

"How much do you think this place is worth?" Brock said as he watched the land roll by from the car window.

"Got to be a few million," Poole answered.

"A pretty good reason for Nora Russell to bump Lake off then."

"Only if she had the capital to buy out his half."

"Buy it from who, though, Poole? We can't find a next of kin, no one seems to stand to inherit."

Poole nodded thoughtfully as they pulled up in the immaculate farmyard.

"We'll see if Nora knows of any family Lake might have had," Brock continued. "Might put a bit of pressure on her in any case, but let's start with Harold Olsen."

Poole had run through the rest of the guests at the computers back at the station and discovered nothing of note on any of them. Matilda Heck had worked as a web designer for a number of London firms before starting out with her own company. They were a small team who apparently hired freelancers when required and according to their last annual accounts, this happened a lot. All in all, the company seemed to be doing well.

Glenn Weaver and Rosa Briggs had joined soon after the company was formed, both straight from university, where Glenn had studied web design and Rosa business and administration. Although it had surprised Brock to know that the bulk of Matilda's employees had been hired without experience, he was the first to admit that he had no idea what the norms of the industry were.

It was Harold Olsen who had really piqued their interest though. Poole had discovered that he had worked as an investment broker in the city at the same time as Lake and had been fired around the same time as the other had quit. Combined with the argument he'd had with Lake the day before his death, Brock had one of those feelings that suggested there was something there worth poking at.

"Sirs," Sanders said as she greeted them at the door as she had done before. "We've had an incident."

"What is it, Sanders?" Brock asked.

"Well, sir, we've had a bit of a fight," she said as she turned, leading them into the building.

"A fight?! Who the bloody hell has been fighting?!"

"Rosa Briggs walloped Matilda Heck, Sir. Quite a right hook on her, that one."

"And do we know why she did this?"

"Wouldn't say, Sir, she's in here," she indicated a side room.

"Ok, well, I guess we better start with her instead. Can I ask how a fight managed to break out when you and Davies were supposed to be watching them?"

"It was all a bit sudden, Sir," she answered in a slightly affronted tone. "They were all talking calmly, and then Briggs just leapt at her."

"Alright, alright," Brock sighed and followed Poole into her room as he pushed the door open.

Rosa Briggs was sitting on what was clearly a

massage table, set into the centre of a room containing nothing else other than shelves of towels and candles that lined the walls.

"Now then, Miss Briggs, what's been going on while we've been away?" Brock said once he and Poole were standing before her.

"It was just a disagreement," she said, her head bowed towards her feet, which dangled from the table she was sitting on as though she was a schoolgirl in trouble in front of a stern teacher.

"A disagreement that ended with you punching your boss in the face?"

"You wouldn't understand," she said as she burst into tears, and buried her head in her hands. "That woman is the bloody devil!"

Brock exchanged glances with Poole, whose pen was hovering above his notepad, paused by this sudden outburst.

"Then why don't you explain it to us," Poole said in what Brock had come to recognise as his "getting them to talk" voice. It was soft and reassuring, but not one of pity. It was a tone designed to suggest that there was a sympathetic ear that would understand your problems. "Designed" was, in Brock's mind, the wrong word. Poole put no thought or effort into the move. It was as natural to him as his deep-rooted desire to apologise for things constantly.

Rosa lifted her head and removed her hands from the sharp cheekbones that gave her such a striking appearance.

"Matty," she spat the name as though it was an insult, "only ever wants what she can't have."

"And what was it she wanted from you?" Poole asked. "Glenn?"

Brock raised an eyebrow at this leap of guesswork and raised the second at the reaction it caused in Rosa.

Her slight body jolted upright from the slouched position she had been in and her eyes flashed with anger.

"Yes! Bloody Glenn!" she snapped. "We're engaged! But that didn't matter to her!"

"They slept together? And was that here at the retreat?" Poole pushed.

Her eyes glazed briefly. "No, this was months ago."

Brock watched his partner frown. "And today you confronted her about it?"

"No, we had it all out at the time. She called me into her office one day and told me outright, said she was sorry and that it had been a mistake." She shook her head as fresh tears appeared in her eyes. "She treated it as though it was just some hiccup at work, like an admin error we could just correct and move on from. She knew exactly what she was doing though. She didn't call me in there to apologise, she called me in to gloat. She wanted to watch me crumble."

"And what happened today?" Brock asked, getting impatient to get to the point where it became relevant to the case at hand.

"Today?!" Rosa shrieked, "today she bloody well did it again!"

"She slept with Glenn again? This morning?" Poole asked, incredulous.

"No! She ..." the young woman paused, her eyes glancing between the two men in front of her.

"This is a murder enquiry," Brock said in a low tone. "We need to know everything, Miss Briggs, and anything you might hold back could either let a killer go free or implicate yourself."

She bit her bottom lip as her hands came together in her lap, her right hand turning the engagement ring on her left hand.

Brock glanced at Poole and raised one finger from where his hand rested on his knee, a signal to wait. Sometimes the best thing you could do when trying to get information from a witness was just give them a little time, a little silence.

There was a knock on the door and Brock gave a

grunt of annoyance before shouting out "Yes?" In an annoyed tone.

The door opened to reveal Constable David Davies, his face pale and his Adam's apple bobbing in his neck like a yo-yo. "Um, Sir? I think I better talk to you for a moment."

Brock rolled his eyes, but got up and moved out through the door.

"What is it, Davies? I'm in the middle of an interrogation!"

"I know, Sir, and I'm sorry, but it's Matilda Heck. She's gone, Sir."

CHAPTER THIRTEEN

"Gone? What do you mean gone?"

Davies shifted uncomfortably from foot to foot. "After Miss Briggs had punched her, she went upstairs to the bathroom and her room. She said she needed a lie-down."

"And you let her go on her own?"

"Well, yes, Sir. She had a nosebleed, seemed only normal she would want to go and sort it out. Then Sanita got here, and I told her to check on her in her room and she wasn't there."

"Bloody hell," Brock muttered before turning and opening the door behind him. He leaned in. "We will pick up this interview later, Miss Briggs," he said to the young woman who was still sitting quietly with knees tucked together as he had left her. "Poole? We need to look around upstairs."

Poole frowned, but rose and followed him as he headed towards the central staircase of the building.

"Where's Sanders now?" Brock asked Davies

"She's upstairs, Sir," he answered nervously.

"And have any of the other guests gone walkabout?"

"No, Sir!" Davies squawked, "None of them have moved!"

"Alright," Brock sighed, "get back to the guests and this time make sure none of them goes anywhere until we get back," Brock called over his shoulder to Davies who called back an affirmative before dashing off.

"Matty Heck went upstairs for a lie-down and has apparently vanished," Brock said, slightly breathlessly as they rushed up the steps.

Poole didn't answer but increased the speed in which he was taking the steps next to Brock and overtook him.

They arrived at a landing that ran to their left and right and was dotted with doors.

"Sir," Poole said, pointing to the far left of the hallway where a fire door was slightly ajar.

They moved quickly down the hallway and stepped out of the door, which led down a metal staircase to the ground. Constable Sanita Sanders was halfway down it and staring out across the grounds that lay before them.

"There's no trace of her, Sir," she said, turning to them and climbing back up the stairs, which rang with a metallic sound at each step. "I'm sorry, I was out the front calling into the station and when I came back in Davies had let her go up. I waited a few minutes and then went up to check on her, but she was gone."

"How long do you think it was before she came up and you followed?" Poole asked.

"Probably only about twenty minutes," she answered, looking out across the grounds again. "I think there might be a road over there," she said, pointing to a distant hedgerow.

"Poole, call the station. Get everyone on the lookout for her in Bexford and the surrounding area. I don't think there's much hope of us catching her now if she made it to the road, but we need to try. Also, put a call into London and give them her details. They can send someone around to her address, see if she heads back there."

Poole nodded and lifted the phone to his ear, leaning against the railing and looking out over the grounds beneath them.

"Come on," Brock said to Sanders before turning

back inside. "You might as well show me the rooms while we're up here."

"These two belong to Nora Russell and Christopher Lake," she said, pointing to the first two doors which were opposite each other in the corridor.

Brock opened the one on the right and peered inside.

"Nora Russell only stayed here when they had guests," Sanita continued, "she's got a place in Bexford, but Christopher Lake lived here all the time."

Brock looked around the plain and sparsely furnished room. A double bed, a side table and a chest of drawers with a small mirror above it were all the furniture that was in the room. There were no pictures, no personal possessions. It could have been the room of a monk. Brock wondered if this was all part of the experience of the retreat—a basic, unflashy room in order to give their guests more time for contemplation or some such nonsense.

"Whose room is this?" he asked.

"That's the victim's."

He turned back to her, "And you said he lived here? Bloody hell." He stepped into the room and opened the door of the small wardrobe which were to the left and moved his hand along the robes that hung there before closing it again and stepping out of the room. He moved across to the opposite door and opened it. There were a few more personalised touches here, but they were all related to the business. A small desk with rows of files on top which ran along against the wall. Shelves held more folders interspersed with books.

"And I guess this is Nora Russell's room, then?" he said thoughtfully.

"Yes, Sir."

They moved on. Matty Heck's room was next. Again there was the same basic setup as in Christopher Lake's room and no personal items.

"Apparently the guests are told not to bring anything, they even have to surrender their mobiles."

"Wouldn't she have had some toiletries at least?" Brock asked as he opened the wardrobe, "and clothes?"

"She definitely had clothes, she must have grabbed them. Her suitcase is gone as well. No beauty products though, they all had to use special natural products that are provided for them in the communal bathrooms."

"By communal you mean...?"

She smiled at him, "No, Sir, they weren't all in there together at the same time. There are three bathrooms, all with locks, at the end of the corridor. They shared them."

He nodded and continued. Rosa Briggs' room was next, the same simple furniture. He noted the single bed.

"Did Rosa Briggs and Glenn Weaver have individual rooms?"

"Yes Sir, there is a strict 'no funny business' rule here."

Brock snorted, "Maybe that's why Miss Briggs was so upset." They moved to the opposite wall where Glenn Weaver and Harold Olsen had rooms; theirs had barely anything of note, save the odd book.

Poole had returned from the fire escape and had followed them down the corridor, peering into the rooms himself as he passed.

"Nothing, Sir?" he asked as he reached them just as they closed the last door.

"Nothing," Brock answered with a sigh. He heaved up his trousers and moved back towards the staircase. "Come on, we need to ask Nora Russell where she thinks Matty Heck might have gone from that road." They headed back down the stairs and this time turned left and headed back to the large room that the remaining guests were gathered in.

"Miss Russell," Brock barked, not caring if this news was made public. "Matty Heck seems to have vanished from upstairs and the fire escape door was open. Any idea where she could have gone?" Brock noticed the effect this news had had on Davies, whose face paled as he leaned on a sideboard for support.

The effects on the rest of the party were even more pronounced. Brock watched closely as the employees of Comet Design went wide-eyed in disbelief that their boss could have run at such a moment. Nora Russell, though, looked more than shocked. She looked horrified.

"What?! She's gone?!"

"That's what I said," Brock continued. "I assume she has a car here?"

"If she did, she didn't use it," Nora said, regaining some poise as she pointed towards the large windows which overlooked the farmyard at the front of the building, "we would have seen. No one's left and her car is still there."

"Well, believe me, she's not here now," Brock said gruffly. "We think there's a road to the south of the hedge line, the direction your room overlooks, Miss Russell. Can you tell me if there's any way to access the road from here?"

"There are a couple of gates and stiles along the hedge line," she answered.

"Yeah," Glenn Weaver added, "We were all walking out that way yesterday, and we passed a few of them."

"And did Matty say anything at the time?"

"No," he said shrugging and looking around at the others.

"And none of you had any clue that she might be about to run?"

There was a murmur of negative answers.

"And so I guess none of you has a clue why she's gone either?"

"It's obvious, isn't it?" Rosa Briggs said, folding her arms.

"Rosa," Glenn said in a harsh tone next to her.

"She obviously killed Moonlake and has run away now you've turned up."

Brock eyed the small group, all of whom looked either thoughtful or shocked. He decided to test their commitment to the validity of their statements.

"And how exactly would she have done that, Miss Briggs? Wasn't she sitting here with you all the entire time?"

There were more glances between all the group apart from Rosa Briggs, who glared defiantly back at him, and Nora Russell who was standing to one side impassively.

No one spoke.

"Constable Sanita," Brock said, his eyes still on the group, "go and look along the hedge line. I doubt there will be any trace of her, but we must check."

Sanita nodded and headed for the main doors, pausing to say something quietly to Poole on her way.

Brock waited for her to go and then addressed his sergeant, "Let's go and check all the outbuildings."

"Is that really necessary?" Nora said in a sharp tone. "Your officers have already been over everything."

"That was before someone involved in a murder enquiry disappeared," Brock answered flatly.

"It's clear to anyone that she made it to the road and then went off somewhere," she continued unabated. "She's not anywhere here anymore."

Brock stared at her for a moment. "Well, despite how remarkably informed you seem to be, Miss Russell, we will still be looking. Perhaps you could go and wait at the front door for us? I think it would be a good idea for you to join us."

He turned and nodded to Poole for him to follow. They moved back through the house to the other wing of the building and entered the meditation room they had been using for the interrogations.

"Bring up one of your map things on your phone, will you Poole? I want to get an aerial view of the place."

Poole nodded, pulled his phone from his pocket and began to tap away on it. Brock watched him, feeling slightly impotent. He had never grasped the worldwide web at its inception, but as the devices had become smaller and more complicated in what seemed like the blink of an eye, the idea of him ever being able to catch up seemed ever more distant. He had decided that this was what delegation was for, and when possible, he never touched a computer or smartphone unless it was to move it out of the way to place his coffee down.

"You could get onto any one of three major roads," Poole said. Brock moved around behind him and peered over his shoulder at the map on the small screen where the road that ran along the opposite side of the hedge ran clear across the screen. Poole pinched on it and it zoomed out to show how it connected to a series of small country roads that spread out in all directions.

"She could have gone anywhere if she'd got the road, but she'd still need a car," Brock said, "or at least someone to meet her on the road with one," he added, remembering that hers was still on the driveway. "But how could she have arranged for them to get her when there are no phones here?"

Poole closed the map and turned to him. "Sanita allowed Nora to give their mobiles back," he said with a sigh. "They were in a drawer in the office, but they had been processed so she didn't see the harm and it kept them all quiet for a bit."

"Well," Brock sighed, pulling up his trousers, "between her and Davies we may well have lost our killer."

"And perhaps any link we might have had between this case and mum's kidnapping," Poole said in a soft, quiet voice, as though the air had been sucked out of him.

Brock paused and made a mental note not to be too harsh on his two young constables. Poole needed his friends right now, they needed to stay together.

They had to get to the bottom of this case quickly. So far the only lead they had, the only time anything even remotely promising had happened since she had disappeared, was her name being in the appointment book of this place. He was determined to find out if there was any connection that could help find her.

CHAPTER FOURTEEN

"Come on," he said to Poole. "Let's go and check the outbuildings around the yard. Whatever Nora Russell thinks, there's a good chance she has just gone for a wander, or..." he paused, the thought occurring to him for the first time, "maybe something happened to her."

"You mean the killer could have got to her?" Poole said, catching on.

"It's a thought, isn't it? Maybe she saw something she shouldn't have, maybe she was in on it somehow with someone else and they decided to get rid of their partner?"

They both fell silent as they pondered on this.

"Come on," Brock said breaking the silence. "Let's get out there and have a look around."

Poole nodded and followed out of the room and

back towards the entrance of the farmhouse where Nora Russell was standing, hovering nervously.

"Have you heard anything?" she asked as they approached.

"No, not as yet," Brock answered. "Are the buildings around the yard outside unlocked?"

She blinked. "She hasn't gone in there," she answered, "I told you, she headed towards the back road."

"And how can you suddenly be so sure, Miss Russell?"

"I've remembered something from yesterday, she was asking me about that road and if you can get to it from the grounds."

Brock and Poole exchanged glances.

"And you didn't think of this until now?" Poole said.

Brock considered the tone in his partner's voice far more polite than his would have been.

"Yes, it was only when you mentioned the back road. It must have triggered something and then I remembered while I was waiting for you."

There was a skipped beat as she turned between the two of them.

"Nonetheless," Brock said, "we would like to see in those buildings."

"Well, if you must," she said haughtily. "I'll need to get the keys from the office."

"We'll wait," Brock answered.

She hesitated again for a moment as though about to say something else when she turned suddenly and headed off in the direction of the office.

"Is it just me, or do you find her a little reluctant to let us see into these other buildings of hers, Poole?"

"I do, Sir," Poole said thoughtfully "but uniform has checked everything already and found nothing."

"Which makes you wonder why she's so jumpy now all of a sudden, doesn't it? Maybe she's done away with Matty Heck after all and has her in there somewhere."

"Davies said no one else moved though, Sir," Poole reminded him.

Brock exhaled. "Yes, Poole, It seems like everyone on this case has been standing stock still in full sight of everybody else until they do go out of sight, at which point they're either murdered or vanish." Something tickled at the back of Brock's brain as he registered his own words, but before he could think about what it was or Poole could answer, Nora Russell returned.

"I have the keys," she said brusquely as she stepped out of the door.

"Shouldn't we look through the buildings on our own, Sir?" Poole whispered as they followed her across the yard in the now light of the afternoon.

"No," he replied. "I want to see her reaction to us looking around. There's something bothering her about us snooping around here and I want to know what it is."

Poole nodded, and they continued in silence until they came to the first outbuilding. Nora opened the door with one of the keys from the bunch and led them inside.

"These are all still being renovated," She said, gesturing at the piles of wooden planks and bricks that littered the floor. Electrical wires hung from the ceiling and the windows at the rear of the building, unglazed and covered in a waterproof membrane, flapping in the breeze.

"Not very secure," Poole said, pointing at the openings.

"No one has come in or out, I can assure you of that. Your officers checked all the windows at the back when they arrived and I let them in to look around here."

"But have the windows been checked since Matty Heck vanished?" Brock asked, already knowing the answer.

"No, but you surely can't think that she would try to escape by climbing into a sealed room through a window? She'd be trapped!"

"I can see you've put some thought into it," Brock said as he moved around the room. "And what were the plans for these buildings?"

"We were planning for them to be more accommodation, we only have the bedrooms in the house at the moment and this would have allowed us to expand the business hugely."

"But there's no work happening at the moment?" he said, glancing back at her.

"No," she said, pulling at her tweed jacket to straighten it. "We've paused the renovations while we review our financial commitment to the project."

"You mean you ran out of money?" Brock said.

She stared daggers at him. "We were assessing things, the initial work had cost more than expected."

Brock nodded. "Come on, let's look at the others."

They moved on through the various sheds and rooms that surrounded the yard, but nothing revealed anything further as to the possible location of Matty Heck. As they walked back across the yard to the house, the sound of sirens rang in the distance—back up for the search was on the way. Brock knew though that it would be fruitless. He agreed with Nora, Matty Heck had vanished along the back road and was now in the wind.

CHAPTER FIFTEEN

After they had poked and prodded through the various outbuildings, they had met Sanita who was returning to the house from her trip to the hedge line. She reported that there was indeed a small gateway towards the middle with a stile next to it and a few hundred yards on either side another two stiles where someone could access the road. There had been no trace of Matty Heck, and no sign of any car that might have been there to pick her up.

With this disappointing news Brock had attempted to rustle up some coffee, but apparently, all stimulants were strictly banned from the premises and so he had made do with a glass of tap water and was now sitting back in the makeshift interrogation/meditation room in a thoroughly bad mood.

"So, Miss Briggs," he said gruffly. "Shall we pick up where we left off?"

"Why are you in here bothering me when you should be out there catching Matty?" the woman said in a somewhat sulky tone.

"We have plenty of people looking for her now," Poole replied.

Brock recognised that his sergeant was jumping in to stop Brock from being too aggressive. His bad mood must be oozing off him like a bad smell.

"Earlier," Poole continued, "we were talking about why you had punched your boss in the face?"

"Not exactly a wise career move," Brock added, unable to help himself.

"You think I care about this stinking job now?" Rosa snapped, clearly not feeling any calmer since their last discussion with her. "I wouldn't work for that woman again, not ever!" She paused and looked at them both. "Do you think she killed Moonlake? Do you think that's why she's run away?"

"Is there any reason you think she might have killed Mr Lake?" Poole asked.

The young woman frowned and stared at her hands as they rested in her lap. "I don't know, maybe he saw sense and rejected her?" she said with a snap in her voice.

"Rejected her?" Poole said as Brock exchanged

glances with him. "Do you think Miss Heck might have been romantically interested in Mr Lake?"

Rosa laughed, "Well he had a pulse, didn't he? Matty didn't care about anything as long as she made her conquest." For a moment the anger had returned in a flash, but it had vanished just as quickly to be replaced with a sudden sadness. A tear rolled down her left cheek.

"I was so bloody stupid," she said shaking her head before looking up and sighing. "Moonlake was... different," she said in a quiet voice. "He knew I was hurting, he tried to help me. He was a good listener, and I just needed someone to rant to, and he was there for me. He just listened until I had nothing left to say. Then I was thinking about what Glenn had done to me and I just wanted to get my own back, so I thought I'd sleep with Moonlake and rub it in Glenn's face."

"And did you?" Poole asked.

"No," she said, her voice even quieter. "Moonlake was a good bloke. He said that I wasn't in the right place to make that kind of decision. He just held me. We were just sitting there for hours, with him just holding me."

There was a silence as she lost herself in thought, remembering the moment. Brock and Poole both waited until, eventually, she lifted her head and continued.

"When I left his room, Matty saw me and gave me one of her awful looks. I could just bloody tell she was going to tell Glenn, or at least hold it over me for a while. That's the kind of person she is, but I wasn't expecting what she actually did."

"And what was that?" Poole asked.

"She bloody slept with him! With Moonlake! The very next night!" she shouted, the words coming out in a tumbled rush. "I got up for a glass of water in the night and saw her coming out of his room and going back to her own."

She shook her head in frustration and fell silent. When she spoke next, it was in a low, almost whispered voice. "She had already made me look an idiot with Glenn, and now she was doing it again. She just didn't care."

"Did you talk to her? Confront her?" Poole asked.

"Yes," she said quietly. "She laughed at me," she said shaking her head again. "She bloody laughed at me."

CHAPTER SIXTEEN

"So, Mr Olsen," Brock said when they were back, settled into their makeshift interrogation room in the house, "It appears that you weren't quite being honest with us before."

Olsen's mouth hung open, revealing the two large front teeth which put Brock in mind of a rodent. His hand reached up and ran over what little fuzz of hair was left on his head.

"I knew this would happen," he said in a shaky voice. "And now Matty's run off and," He paused and looked up. "She has just run off, hasn't she? I mean, nothing has happened to her, has it?"

"That's an interesting question, Mr Olsen," Brock said gravely.

Olsen's eyes widened in panic. "I didn't mean

anything by it, it's just... someone's been killed, haven't they?"

Brock let the pause lengthen as Olsen squirmed before answering. "At the moment, Mr Olsen, we don't know what has happened to Miss Heck."

"Bloody hell," Olsen said, swallowing.

Brock took the opportunity to glance at Poole and raise his right hand a few inches from his knee where it rested to signal that his partner should remain silent for the moment.

"So come on, Mr Olsen, tell us everything and then things might go a little better for you."

The little man sighed and raised his head.

"I swear, I don't know anything about what's happened or what's going on. I just make the accounts look ok, I didn't want to get involved in all this."

"And what do you mean by 'all this', Mr Olsen?"

His eyes darted between them. "I mean Moonlake dying, Matty vanishing..." his voice trailed off.

Brock nodded. When he had started the interview, the intention had been to press Olsen on his potential past with the victim, Christopher Lake. Now though, it seemed clear that Olsen was more concerned with the financial irregularities at the company he worked for. The others could wait.

"I don't think that is what you meant, Mr Olsen. Can I remind you that this is a potential murder enquiry and as such, if you are found lying to us then the consequences could be very serious indeed."

Olsen gulped, and his head dropped.

"I knew something wasn't right," he said softly, "but I just kept my head down and worked as well as I could. I didn't have any choice," he whined.

"Matty Heck threatened you?"

He looked surprised. "No, Matty didn't threaten me. She gave me a job when no one else would bloody touch me!"

"And why was that?"

Olsen closed his eyes and leaned back in his chair.

"Because I messed up, lost a load of client money and then tried to get myself out of it, and of course, just ended up digging an even bigger hole. I was laid off and badmouthed in the industry in such a way that was pretty sure I wasn't going to get another role in finance. Then I met Matty. She said she was starting up a new company and that she needed someone to handle the finances. It was a big step down, but it was a lifeline."

"How did you meet her?"

"It was random." He laughed, his mood lightening briefly. "I'd gone to try to get an old colleague of mine to help me out, and she was just there in the bar. We got talking," he shrugged.

Brock couldn't help noticing that when the man talked about Matty, there was a sparkle in his otherwise dull eyes. Added to the fact that Miss Heck wasn't the shy and retiring type when it came to flirting, he decided to take a stab in the dark.

"Are you and Matty Heck having a relationship?"

"What? No!" he cried, his cheeks flushing. "She's just a friend. A colleague," he added, fidgeting in his seat.

"So it didn't bother you that she slept with Christopher Lake?"

"What?" he replied, looking as though he had been slapped. "She..? No, I don't believe it."

"Rosa Briggs caught them," Brock said with a certain amount of artistic license. He wanted to push Olsen as much as he could.

"That bastard!" the small man suddenly shouted, rising from his chair. "Hadn't he already taken enough from me?!"

As soon as the words had left his lips, it was clear he regretted them. He looked down at the two detectives in front of him, his eyes widening in a panic, not for the first time in this interview.

"And what else had Christopher Lake taken from you?" Brock asked, an eyebrow rising.

Olsen's mouth opened twice and then closed again, like a goldfish that had inexplicably found itself thrown from its bowl and lay flapping on the coffee table. Eventually, his body sagged in defeat.

"I did know Christopher before this trip," he said sullenly.

"How?"

"When he was working back in the city," he continued. "I met him at one of the bars the investors used to all hang out in." He gave a small, rather humourless laugh. "The same one I met Matty in, actually."

"So, you and Lake were friends?"

"No, we weren't bloody friends! He was the reason I was fired!" he snapped, his lip curling in anger. Again, he sagged as he continued, the flash of fury leaving him. "I'd spoken to him a couple of times, nothing much more than passing the time of day after a long day at work, but then one day he told me he had some information on a particular stock." He looked up at them shiftily.

"Insider trading?" Brock said flatly, remembering the term from a Hollywood film he had watched a few months ago.

"Look, it happens all the time when you're in the

trade. You hear things and you pass on a little nod to your mates and hope they'll do the same for you one day."

"We looked up your record, you don't have a conviction for anything like that, so how did you lose your job?"

"Funnily enough, you only tend to get convicted if you have information that actually makes you money," Olsen said miserably. "The tip Lake gave me backfired."

"And you lost some of your firm's money?"

"Some? I wish. He'd just been so bloody sure. He said it was a once in a lifetime opportunity. I got greedy, used every bit of client money I could get together without anyone noticing and ploughed it all in just before the thing went up in smoke. The company kept it quiet and covered my tracks."

"Why would they do that?"

"The damage to their reputation would have been worse if it came out, clients would never trust them again even if they made a show of me publicly. So they moved me on quietly, but not before spreading the word that I was poison first so I couldn't get another job."

"So when you realised your new firm was working for Lake, you must have been pretty furious," Poole said. "Did you decide to get your revenge then?"

"No! This is why I didn't say anything before because I knew you'd think I had something to do with him dying! The others will tell you though, I never moved from that bloody beanbag all morning. We did a big yoga session yesterday afternoon and I'm in agony today. I was taking the chance to rest. None of us moved and no one else went into that room, Lake must have committed suicide."

Brock stared back at him, but the man's face was blank. He had the eyes of someone who had already revealed his worst and now had nothing more to fear.

CHAPTER SEVENTEEN

B rock sighed and rubbed his face with his hands.

"I need coffee," he said gruffly.

"You need to go home," Poole said leaning back in his chair and swivelling towards him. "Sir," he added, catching the look on his superior's face.

Brock looked at his watch and thought of Laura. She would be at home now and he pictured her cuddling their dog Indy on the sofa, his head resting on her belly where their unborn child grew. He had taken to using her stomach as a cushion almost from the moment she had become pregnant; dogs seemed to be able to sense these things.

"Soon enough," he said, shaking the image from his head, "let's just go over everything again."

Poole turned back to his desk and pulled up his

notebook where he had jotted down the various points they had worked through since they had returned from the retreat.

"Let's start with Matty Heck. When we first looked at her background, nothing jumped out in particular, but now we've gone into the company's accounts a bit more deeply, things look fishy. Lots of small companies paying Heck's web company a strangely large amount of money."

Brock nodded thoughtfully, "so we think there may not be something entirely above board about these business arrangements?"

"Exactly," Poole continued, "And the websites aren't even much to look at, and the companies they've made them don't even seem to have needed them. For instance, two of their customers were laundrettes."

"Right," Brock answered confidently, though, in truth, he still wasn't sure what anyone used websites for. He avoided them like the plague.

"So we need to look into these other companies, see if they're a front for something else. Pass it on to our colleagues in London, see what they come back with."

Poole nodded. "Then there's Olsen's story about losing his job because he lost a load of money.

Someone at the company confirmed it, but they told me to be discreet," he said with a small smile.

"And what about the finances at the retreat?"

"Well, Nora Russell may have been economical with the truth when she was showing us the renovations. She said they were reviewing their financial commitment to the project, but I think that's code for 'we ran out of money' as there's not much in the bank account. Nothing seems particularly off there, though. I've reached out to their accountants to see if they can shed any further light, but the person who handles their account is away on holiday. They gave us the basics, but until he's back, we won't get much else."

"So if we can't find a next of kin for Lake the company will be sold off and Nora will get her 49% share. There's still motive there."

"Agreed, but with Matty suddenly vanishing, she's got to be the prime suspect."

"And Sanders and Davies are sure that no one left when they were with them other than Matty?"

"They are," Poole nodded. "None of the others could have got to her, she must have run."

"Ok, well I guess we better head home," Brock said, rising from his desk. "Ron will be back tomorrow to start looking at the body and we'll get back over to the retreat and start looking at the office where he died again."

"I'm staying at my flat tonight," Poole said quietly. "You and Laura have been really kind, but I need to be at home now."

Brock sighed and walked to the side of his partner who was still sitting in his chair and placed a large hand on his shoulder.

"You know I think it's dangerous, but you know your own mind. Just be careful and keep your phone by you."

"Yes, Sir."

CHAPTER EIGHTEEN

Brock walked into the small hallway of his house feeling more tired than he had done in years. The weight and stress of the last few days since Jenny Poole's disappearance weighing down on him as though he were wrapped in chains.

"Sam?" Laura called from the kitchen.

"Poole's not staying here tonight," he called back In reply as he headed towards the kitchen. "He's gone back to the... Oh, Jack." He paused as he entered the kitchen and saw Jack Poole sitting at the table.

"Hi Sam," Jack said, rising from his seat and extending a hand.

Brock shook it before turning and embracing Laura who had moved across to him from the oven

where she was stirring what he hoped, with a sudden pang of hunger, was their dinner.

"Jack has some information on Jenny," Laura said, placing one hand round Brock's broad shoulders as he took a seat opposite his partner's father and looked at him expectantly.

"Someone was asking around about a location," Jack said, stroking his stubbled chin with his right hand.

"A location?"

Jack nodded. "Somewhere quiet, remote. Somewhere he wouldn't be disturbed..."

"A place where you could hold someone who's been kidnapped," Brock said.

"Exactly. Now no one I know spoke to the guy directly, and we don't know if he got an answer or not, but once I'd heard this I started asking around."

Brock felt the familiar thrill of a potential break in the case. He leaned forward expectantly. "And did you get anything?"

"Not much, but we know he had red hair and seemed..." he paused as he looked up at the Brock, his blue eyes narrowed. "Word is, he seemed unhinged. He freaked people out, and these aren't the kind of people to freak out easily."

Jack's face had paled as he spoke, his voice thickening with emotion. Brock, not for the first

time, wondered how much he still cared for his ex-wife.

"Well," he said, folding his arms, "it's something, and everything helps. Not to mention that I think this means Jenny is alive, you don't worry about a quiet, out of the way place unless you're planning on using it for a while."

"But still no contact from whoever took her," Jack said.

There was something in his tone, something decisive, something ominous, that made the hair on the back of Brock's neck stand up.

"I hope you're not thinking of doing anything stupid, Jack?"

"What can I do?" Jack shrugged. The two men looked at each other for a moment before Jack rose from his chair. "If Guy is back at his flat, I'll put someone outside to keep an eye on him."

"You can do that?" Brock said, somewhat surprised.

"You'd be surprised what I can do when I put my mind to it," Jack answered with a faint smile which faded into a serious, stone-faced look. "You will look after him, won't you, Sam?"

Brock nodded. "As much as I can," he replied, his thoughts straying to previous colleagues he'd lost. The cursed bloody detective, he thought bitterly.

"Whatever happens," Jack continued as he moved towards the door. Brock turned to him with Laura by his side. "I want you to make sure that he's ok. I always knew that boy deserved better than me." He looked between the two of them and smiled. "And now I think he has it." He turned and walked out into the hall. Brock followed him quickly, something worrying him about the finality of this brief exchange.

"If you know something that you're not telling me..." he said, his voice booming around the confined space.

Jack turned back to him with one hand on the front door handle. "I don't know anything new, and if I did, I would tell you."

"Then tell me what is going on," Brock demanded. "Why this sudden talk of me looking after Guy?"

Jack smiled. "You're going to be a good father when your little one comes along," he answered, before turning and stepping out into the night.

CHAPTER NINETEEN

P oole slumped back onto his sofa, drank deeply from the beer he clutched in his hand and closed his eyes.

Three days. How could it have been that long already? The time seemed to have passed in a blur and yet, at the same time, it seemed like forever since he had heard his mother's voice, seen her smile, and had her drive him mad with her latest crazy plan for spiritual fulfilment.

She had been due to go to the retreat, that was something. The two cases had to be related. It was too much of a coincidence. He knew what that meant for his mother's chances of being found alive and well. If someone had been willing to murder Christopher Lake in cold blood, then who's to say that they wouldn't have done the same if his mother had got in the way? There had been a moment, just a fleeting one, back at the retreat where he had even wondered if his mother had committed the crime. He couldn't imagine it for a moment. His mother was the type to gently usher a fly out of the flat through an open window rather than swat it, but something still worried away at the back of his mind.

When he had been younger, he would never have imagined his father could have been wrapped up with an illegal drug gang. His best memories were of long summers where Jack would take him to the park and they would play football, fly kites and laugh and laugh. Then one day it was over, and the image he'd had of his father was shattered forever. He couldn't help but wonder if his mother was about to do the same thing, or had already done it.

His phone buzzed next to him and he lifted it to see the message. Sanita, wondering if he wanted her to come around. He quickly tapped out a message saying no before taking another swig of beer and laying back again. He wanted to be alone right now. For the past few days everyone had been so kind, so supportive, so smothering.

He felt a sudden and overwhelming wave of tiredness take over and slipped into a sleep of utter exhaustion.

When he woke several hours later, it was with a

dry mouth and aching back. He quickly lifted the beer bottle which had toppled from his hand on the sofa, saving the last few drops from joining the rest that had soaked into a wide stain on the worn fabric.

As he moved towards the kitchen looking for a cloth, he became aware of the weak light filtering around the edge of his curtains and realised with a panic that it must be morning. He pulled his phone from his pocket to check the time, 5:45am. Good, he wouldn't be late for work, even if he would be tired. He clicked the email icon which showed he had a notification and it opened to show a single line of text.

TWO DOWN, ONE TO GO...

CHAPTER TWENTY

"What do you mean?" Poole said, his eyes wild.

Brock paused, he had to handle this carefully. He had never seen Poole like this; his partner was angry, sad, confused, and more worrying than anything else, unpredictable. The last thing Poole needed was to do something rash that might get someone hurt.

"Your father came to our house last night. I think he thought you would be there."

"And he said something about the case?"

"Yes," Brock answered. "He said someone had been asking around about a remote location he could use."

"And do we know who it was?"

"No, all we had was that it was someone with red hair."

Brock decided to leave out the part where Jack had mentioned the man seeming unhinged. He frowned as he thought of Jack's behaviour. He looked into Poole's eyes, which shone with frightening intensity. "There was something off about Jack though. He told me to look after you, and the way he said it..."

Poole slumped back in his seat, his face pale, as though the words had delivered a physical blow.

To Brock's own ears, the words now sounded even more ominous than they had done last night.

After receiving the message, Poole had called Jack immediately and had been ringing periodically for the last two hours, to no reply. Sharp and Anderson had been handed his phone and had, after Sharp caught Brock's eye, treated the matter with significance. The email was being traced by the cyber-division in London as they spoke.

Now they were in an interview room at the station where Brock had decided they would sit and have a coffee while he explained Jack's visit last night and the peculiar nature of it.

"What do you think he was planning to do?" Poole asked in a hollow voice, all anger and fight suddenly gone from him.

"I don't know," Brock answered, "But I think your father cares for your mother more than we realised, maybe he never really stopped loving her despite everything that's passed between them. I think he tried to find her."

"Well, he's had more bloody luck than we have then hasn't he?" Poole shouted as he slapped the metal table between them.

Brock let the clang ring out into silence and waited a moment before continuing. Partly to give his colleague time to calm a little, and partly because what his partner had said was a reflection of his own worst fears manifesting themselves. The cursed detective moniker he had earned was burning in his mind.

"You know what this means, Poole?"

His partner looked up at him and took a long, deep breath.

"It means they are definitely targeting my family and I'm the next victim."

Brock nodded, glad that he understood, sad that this young man who had been through so much was having to endure more.

"It must be to do with the shooting," Poole said, "but what I don't understand is why it's focused on me. I'm the one they sent the text to when they took Mum, I'm the one they've emailed now they have Dad as well. Why? Why am I the one they want to hurt most?" Tears sprang into his eyes as he bowed his head.

Brock stared at the top of his head, cursing himself for the unease he always felt in situations like this. He had enough trouble dealing with his own emotions, let alone those of other people.

He got up, walked around the desk and rested a hand on Poole's shoulder, In what he realised was fast becoming his signature move and a useless one at that. He said nothing; what was there to say? Poole was right. Someone seemed to be trying to inflict maximum pain on him, and they were taunting him with the capture of his parents.

Jack's disappearance, in particular, was a worry. Brock didn't know exactly what Jack's life since leaving prison entailed, but he knew he wasn't short of protection. He always seemed to have one or two large men with dull, unimaginative eyes around him who followed orders. How could he have been taken? Why had he been alone last night when he had left Brock's home when right now, of all times, he should have been taking extra precautions? Something occurred to Brock like a bullet through the brain, and he swore loudly.

Poole looked up at him in alarm.

"What is it?" he said, wiping his eyes with his hand.

Brock hesitated, unsure whether to share his sudden realisation or not, but faced with his young partner whose face looked up at him with a mixture of hope and fear, the choice was made for him.

"I don't think your father was kidnapped," he said with a sigh.

"But the email?" Poole said in confusion.

"No, I'm sorry, I think the kidnapper has him alright," Brock said quickly, realising he had given Poole false hope. "But I think your father knew what was happening. I think he wanted to be taken."

"What?! But why on earth would he do that?"

"Because of your mother," Brock said softly as he took his seat again. "The way he was talking, making sure I would look after you, talking about your mother. I think he'd already made his decision."

"But how could he have known the kidnapper was going to come for him next?"

"Your father was alone last night. We spoke to his friends earlier, and by that, I mean his heavies, and they said he told them he didn't need them. It's only a guess, but I think Jack spotted that he was being followed and decided he'd make things easy for his attacker. I'd imagine he hoped he would be taken to where your mum was being held."

"But what could he do then? What would be the point?!" Poole cried, throwing his hands in the air.

"It would mean he was with her," Brock said. "Sometimes that's enough for someone you love."

CHAPTER TWENTY-ONE

B rock walked along the corridor in a thoughtful mood. He had ordered Poole to go and have a coffee with Sanders, hoping it would help get his head straight, at least temporarily, while he went to see Ron Smith about the body of Christopher Lake.

He knocked on the office door and took a deep breath as the customary silence rang out before Ron Smith answered. A simple power play that had always annoyed him more than it should.

"Come in," came the familiar weasel voice from inside. Brock opened the door and landed heavily in the chair opposite the small, bald figure of Ronald Smith.

The usual reptilian smile played on his lips as he placed his hands together as though in prayer and touched them to his lips.

"Now then, has there been any news on Pond's mother?"

Brock's jaw clenched at the surely deliberate error.

"I mean," Ron continued, "has she turned up at some hippy festival or something yet? I hear she's quite the type to go flouncing off,"

"Tell me about the body," Brock said flatly. Ron seemed to sense that he was not in the mood to be messed around and so took a folder on the desk to his right and opened it.

"Well, I'm afraid I can't give you much information on the stabbing itself," he said sighing.

"What do you mean?"

"Well there was one clear, deep wound that was what actually did for the fellow, but then someone made a mess of the entry wound with a series of shallower cuts."

Brock frowned. "A second aggressor? Someone not as strong as the person who made the killer blow?"

"That could be the case, but it's really impossible to say. The wound itself is a mess. It looks as though someone just decided to dig a hole in him."

"And they couldn't be the first attempts at him committing suicide, I suppose? Until he finally got it right and plunged the blade in?"

"I can't say for certain, but I would be fairly sure that the deeper wound was made first and the slicing and dicing came afterwards. Not what I would call the usual signs of suicide."

"And the time of death matches with the hour he was locked in the office?"

Ron looked up at him curiously. "Well, of course," he said smiling. "I gather from that question you're struggling to understand how a man in a locked room could have been stabbed in the chest?"

Brock grunted an acknowledgement.

"It is a bit of a puzzle, isn't it?" Ron said in a slightly mocking tone, revelling in Brock's lack of progress. "Unless of course, this murder follows the plot of Murder on the Orient Express and they all did it!" He emitted a jerky cackle that ended in a snort, but Brock's face remained as impassive as stone.

Internally, he was shocked. Although farfetched, this was an actual possibility, and he was horrified that he hadn't considered it. The abduction of Poole's parents had distracted him, had caused him to take his eye off the ball enough that he had missed what was probably the most obvious answer to the whole mystery of how an entire room full of people were somehow oblivious to a murder occurring just feet away from them.

That they were all lying, that they were all involved.

"Is there anything else?" Brock grumbled as he rose from his seat.

"Actually, quite a bit," Ron said, leaning back in his chair and enjoying his colleague's discomfort.

"Out with it then," Brock rumbled.

"I have sent no less than three samples off to the lab to be compared against the DNA swabs your officers took from the suspects at the retreat."

"Where from? From the body?" Brock snapped, impatient at how Smith was teasing out the information.

"I took a sample of skin from under the fingernails of the victim's right hand."

"Defensive wound?"

"I haven't looked at the samples myself yet. I thought it best to get samples off to the lab as soon as possible, but there were no other cuts or abrasions that you would expect from a knife attack."

"OK, what were the other two?"

"I found some hair in the victims clothing, brown going to grey, and wiry, so I would imagine it was from someone older, probably male," he paused as his tongue flicked across his thin lips, "and then there was the most interesting discovery." He leaned back in his chair and placed his hands behind his head.

"So, do you really think Pond's mother has been kidnapped? I mean," he laughed, "they're surely not going to get much of a ransom from him are they?"

"Did you find something that links the two cases?" Brock asked urgently, leaning forward. He knew he had guessed wrongly from the look of surprise which flashed across Smith's face.

"And how could the cases be related, I wonder?" he said in a mocking voice. "Now, let me see, a man who runs a spiritual retreat has been murdered and a woman, who from what I hear was very much into her spirituality has disappeared. I assume you're treating her as a suspect?"

Brock knew he was guessing, throwing things out there just to rile him, which made him even more furious because it was working. He got up suddenly, the chair clattering backwards onto the floor as he planted two large hands on the desk in front of Smith and leaned forward until he was just inches from his face.

"I suggest you tell me what you found before I put that tiny little peanut head of yours through the wall," he growled.

"You... you can't talk to me like that!" Smith answered, his voice quivering.

"Well, you can tell everyone how badly I spoke to

you once you've removed your head from the wall, can't you?"

Ron swallowed and looked back down to the folder in front of him.

"I found something lodged in the victim's mouth," he lifted a small plastic evidence bag from the folder and slid it across the desk.

Brock lifted it to his eye and tried to make sense of the few letters and numbers that were barely legible on the small scrap of paper.

"It's a receipt," Ron said. "I managed to make out the shop name with a magnifying glass and a strong light behind it and it's from a small book shop in Bexford. The address is here on a copy I took of the receipt." He passed Brock a sheet of paper.

"What do you mean it was lodged in his mouth?" Brock asked.

"Just as I say," Ron answered, some of his usual annoying tone returning now his personal space was returned. "It was at the back of the teeth on one side. I can't say how it got there, of course."

"Could the victim have pushed it into his own mouth in the hope we'd find it?" Brock asked.

"You mean in some last-ditch attempt to tell us who the killer was?" Ron smiled, the mocking tone now fully restored. "No, the first blow from the knife would have killed him almost instantly, he wouldn't have been able to scrabble around eating paper afterwards, particularly with the killer still hacking away with the knife."

"Is that everything?"

"Until I get the results from the DNA I sent away, yes."

Brock turned and left the room without another word.

CHAPTER TWENTY-TWO

As Brock crossed the car park back towards the station he saw the broad-shouldered figure of Sergeant Anderson moving through the cars. He picked up his pace and cut him off before he could reach his vehicle.

"Where are you going, Anderson?" he grumbled.

Anderson's face contorted itself to hide the sneer that was attempting to fight its way to the surface.

"We're following up a lead in the missing person case, Sir," he answered flatly, his eyes flicking behind Brock towards the car that he clearly wanted to get to.

"By 'new lead' I take it you mean the fact that Jack Poole has now been taken by the kidnapper as well?"

Anderson raised his chin as he stared back at him.

"Jack Poole is an ex-con who we suspect is still involved in some pretty dodgy practices, Sir."

"And that means that we shouldn't care if someone snatches him from the street?"

"No, Sir, it means that it is hard to know whether he has been snatched at all. We've contacted officials he had contact with after leaving prison and they haven't heard from him, but it wouldn't be the first time an ex-con stopped checking in."

Brock eyeballed him for a moment and was pleased to see that Anderson's defiant air was showing cracks. He still had it in him to stare down some arrogant young idiot with a six-pack.

"So where are you going now?"

"We're going to talk to some," he paused meaningfully before spitting out the next word, "Associates of Jack Poole's, to see if we can put this to bed."

"And where is Sharp?"

"I'm picking him up on the way," he answered stiffly.

"Where from?"

Anderson hesitated again, but something hardened in his expression and a faint smile came to one corner of his mouth.

"Inspector Sharp had an early meeting with the Chief Inspector, Sir. Between you and me, I believe it could be to do with the upcoming vacancy in that position." He had delivered this line with brisk respectfulness which sounded to Brock's ear as though it was being mimicked from the military tones of Sharp. It was clear though that his intentions were to somehow wind up Brock about the promotion.

"I think it's wise, Anderson, for you to start thinking about the kind of person you want to be," Brock said, pulling himself up to his full height and glaring down at Anderson even with his six-foot frame. "Sometimes we can head down a path that seems like the right one for us at the time, only to find that one day you don't like where it's taken you and it's too far back to find another way. Make sure you don't find yourself there, Anderson, because there are no second chances." He pushed past him in the narrow gap between cars, his shoulder knocking Anderson's, who stepped back to keep his balance.

Brock knew what an early morning meeting between Sharp and Tannock meant. It meant a round of golf. Undoubtedly that's where Anderson was now going to pick him up from. They wouldn't investigate thoroughly though. Sharp won't like mixing with the kind of tight-lipped and experienced men that Jack Poole hangs around with. He'd wash his hands of the whole situation as quickly as he could. Brock knew he could put the frighteners on him to stir up a little action, but only Tannock could really make him take the case seriously. However, Tannock was on the verge of retiring and disinterested in messy cases involving one of his own detective's family and now an ex-con. Anderson was going to become one of them. One of the old boys' club who played golf on work time and took the praise for themselves and passed the bad news downwards to subordinates.

Something struck him as he walked back towards the station. He would never be able to change these people, and he would never be able to change the system that continued to produce them, not if he was part of it. He had been shying away from the idea of going for Tannock's job once he retired. Moving away from the investigation side of police work and becoming embroiled in the administrative didn't particularly appeal to Brock, but then, perhaps if he was at the top of the pile he could do things differently? Anderson, despite his appearance, had intelligence. He could be moulded into something useful. Poole was as sharp as a tack and willing to learn, and there was promise in Sanders who he knew had aspirations of her own to make detective. Then there was Laura and their baby. The time would come, he knew, when leaving the house every day to chase down criminals that at any moment could turn up at his house as they had once done at Poole's would become far harder than it had ever been. He had already been concerned at Poole's presence at the house while his family appeared to be being targeted and had felt deeply ashamed by his feelings.

He jogged up the steps to the reception of Bexford police station in a determined mood. Maybe he needed to stop giving into the future and start shaping it. No more cursed detective.

CHAPTER TWENTY-THREE

Brock found Poole still sitting at the canteen table he had left him at earlier with Constable Sanders. They saw him enter, and he nodded at them as he moved to the coffee machine. As he was making the second cup, Poole came to his side.

"What news is there from Ron?"

Brock looked up at him as the coffee machine gurgled and shook next to them. His young partner's face had regained its colour and his jaw was set in a determined fashion. He looked business like, as though he was now focussed on the task ahead of finding his parents rather than dwelling on what might have happened to them.

Poole had picked up on the look of inspection and gave a small smile.

"I'm fine, but I want to crack on with this case.

Who knows if it has anything to do with Mum and Dad, but it's still our only lead."

Brock nodded as the coffee machine rattled to a stop.

"Ok, well let me fill you in on the way back to the retreat." He handed Poole one of the Styrofoam cups as they made their way back out towards the car park.

Sanders was back at her desk as they passed through the main office and Brock noticed the concerned look she gave Poole as they passed.

He knew the two of them had grown close, and he also knew that as a superior officer he should be concerned about how Poole and Sanders' relationship might affect their work and the team as a whole. In the end though, and although he would be loathed to admit it, he was a romantic soul, and he took some pleasure in spotting the stolen glances and body language between them that showed their affection.

"Sir!" a voice rang out as they stepped into the reception. They turned towards the main desk where Roland Hale's considerable bulk was in a state of excitement.

"What is it, Hale?"

"I've just had a call from London. They've picked up Matilda Heck!"

"Good, are they holding her?"

"Yes," Roland said grinning, "because they've got a warrant to go over her place off the back of this murder and they're pretty sure they're going to find a whole bucket-load to charge her with!"

"Explain," Brock said gruffly, walking over and leaning on the desk heavily.

"Well they tried to call through to you, Sir, but when they got no answer, they called the front desk. Apparently, this Matilda has been on their radar for a while. She's designed websites for a load of small companies they suspect of being fronts for gangs in London."

"They think she was money laundering," Poole said as he gave Brock a knowing look.

They had suspected something of the sort earlier, but Brock knew what was playing on his sergeant's mind. Were any of the gangs related to the one his father had been seen to double-cross all those years ago involved with Matty Heck?

"You go back to the office and make some calls," Brock said. "Follow it up and then get the people from the retreat rounded up and brought here. We'll see if we can put a little pressure on them."

"Actually, Sir," Roland said, "I just had a call from Constable Morgan who's down at the retreat and he says," he squinted down at a note on the desk in front of him, "a Nora Russell is insisting that her guests are allowed to leave and go back to London. Apparently, she's causing a bit of a stink about it."

"Right," Brock said slightly puzzled, "Well, I think we'd better see why she's so keen to get rid of them all of a sudden, shouldn't we? Off you go, Poole," he jerked his head back towards the office, "I've got a little errand to take care of and then I'll join you back here."

"Won't you need the car, Sir?" Poole said, frowning.

"I'm going to walk, thank you," Brock answered as he pushed through the station doors and headed out into the air which seemed so fresh after the still, closeness of the station.

His right knee twinged as he used his long stride to eat up the distance between the station and the centre of Bexford. He was getting old, and soon he would be a father. At the back of his mind, he had a nagging doubt about how well he was going to bear up when he was working the often-long hours of police investigation work and then being clambered all over by an enthusiastic toddler when he got home. He smiled to himself. He was looking forward to finding out.

He pulled his phone from his pocket and called his wife.

"Hey, you ok? Any news?" she said quickly as soon as she answered.

"No news and I'm fine," he replied. He could hear the mixture of relief and disappointment in her voice at once. The last few days had been stressful for everyone, and the last thing he wanted was for her to worry.

"How are you feeling?"

"Oh fine, just busy," she answered.

He frowned. He had told her to start taking it easier at her job at the museum, but that was like asking a teenager to cut down on using their phone. It just wasn't going to happen.

"I need to call on your encyclopaedic knowledge of Bexford," Brock said.

"For a case?"

He heard the slight rise of excitement in her voice and smiled. "Yes, for a case. So, Doctor Watson, can you tell me a shop that has the words 'of the east' at the end? I thought it might have been a takeaway at first, but I'm pretty sure I know the name of all those."

Her musical laugh rang down the phone. It still had the ability to send a warm glow through him.

"You definitely know the names of them all," she said in an admonishing tone. "Anyway, it's nothing to do with food, it's got to be the 'Soul of the East', it's on a side street over by the College. It sells bits of Indian and Chinese art and things. I bought you those Chinese worry balls for Christmas from there one year, remember?"

"Oh, yes, of course," Brock answered automatically. As well as an ability to ruin almost any meal she attempted to cook, Laura had a knack for buying presents so ill-suited to the recipient that they invariably ended in a charity shop a few months later.

"How is Guy doing?" Laura asked, her voice tentative, as though she was unsure she wanted to hear the answer.

"It's hard to say," Brock said, sighing. "I think he feels helpless, bloody hell, we all do."

"I just know they're ok," Laura said. "I can feel it. Something will turn up and you'll get to the bottom of it."

"I hope so," Brock answered, his fists clenching as a sudden wave of anger and frustration passed through him.

"It's not your fault," Laura said softly after a moments pause. "You know that, don't you?"

"I know, I'd better go, I'm almost at the college."

"Ok, I've just looked it up, it's on Slip Street to the left of the college entrance."

"Ok thanks, see you later, and take care of yourself."

"I will," Laura said, laughing at his concern, "love you."

"Love you too."

Brock shoved the phone in his pocket as he walked past the glass-fronted building of the college, which was set back from the road. He turned down the road marked Slip Street.

The shop was only a few feet from the main road and barely ten foot across. Its grimy front window was full of brightly coloured silks, wooden carvings and hanging symbols in glass that dangled from its roof. He entered, causing a little bell to chime above him, and looked about. The walls of the square room were lined with shelves, all of which were covered in similar merchandise to the window. Incense burned on the corner of the counter which was covered in papers at the back of the room. He was about to call out when a woman burst through the curtains which hung over the opening in the back wall and stared at him through thick-rimmed glasses.

"Hello! How can I help you?" she said in a deep, booming voice that accompanied her broad smile.

"I'm Detective Inspector Brock and I was wondering if you could confirm that this receipt was from your shop?" He pulled the copy of the receipt Ron had given him and held it out to her.

"Oh, how exciting!" she said as she took the receipt. "I've always wanted to be one of those people who help with enquiries and solve the case, that sort of thing." She squinted and adjusted the glasses as she moved the paper closer and then further away. "Oh yes, definitely one of mine. I can tell you who bought it as well if that's of any use to you?"

"You can? Who was it?"

"A girl called Rosa came in yesterday all keen to know about yoga. I sold her a book on it, and we got chatting. Strange girl, I thought."

"Why do you say that?"

"Oh, just that I got the impression she wasn't really interested. Got the impression she was just trying to learn a list of facts rather than actually really know anything about it if you know what I mean?"

CHAPTER TWENTY-FOUR

"Are my suspects in interrogation?" Brock asked as he entered the reception of Bexford Police Station.

"No, Sir, they're still back at the retreat," Roland answered from behind the desk.

"What? Why?" Brock thundered.

Roland swallowed and took a step back from the desk.

"Someone's been throwing bricks through windows in town and one of them went through the Conservative Club, so the Chief Inspector wanted some uniform on the streets straight away."

"And what the bloody hell has that got to do with getting my suspects here?"

"Not enough people or cars, Sir, but don't worry, as soon as they've made a bit of a presence in town they'll be out to scoop up your lot at the retreat. Davies is out there with them now keeping an eye on them."

Brock swore under his breath and headed through to the main office where he was immediately struck by the quiet efficiency that seemed to be settled over the space. He spotted the reason in the corner. Chief Inspector Clive Tannock was standing with arms folded, his bulbous and forever-red nose turned downwards with one hand on his chin in a thoughtful pose as Inspector Sharp spoke in a low voice next to him.

Sharp's eyes caught Brock's, and he said something that caused the Chief Inspector to look up. Brock deliberately averted his gaze and headed towards the back door in the room which led to his office, but the two men moved across to cut him off.

"Ah, Brock," Tannock said, "I wonder if I can have a quick word with you in my office?"

"I'm rather busy, Sir," Brock rumbled.

"Aren't we all? Still, I'd like a word," Tannock said before leading the way through the door and to his office at the end of the corridor, with Sharp heading back to his own office.

"Now, Brock," Tannock said as he landed heavily in the leather chair on the opposite side of the desk from where Brock took a seat. "How are things going on this case of yours? Sounds like a suicide, doesn't it?"

"I don't think so, Sir, no."

"Oh?" Tannock said in mild surprise. "Sharp tells me the victim was found in a locked room, no other way out and witnesses that say no one came or went?"

"With all due respect, Sir," he replied in a voice he tried hard to keep respectful, "neither you or Sharp have been to the scene or interviewed the suspects. Also, people don't tend to kill themselves with a knife to the chest."

"So you have a clear idea of who the murderer is?"

"Not yet, Sir, it's still too early to say."

"Then surely you must at least know how the killer got in and out of this sealed room without anyone seeing?"

Brock stared at the grey eyes of the man in front of him. He knew he wasn't exactly a bad sort, by all accounts he had even been a decent detective in his day. Now though, his mind lay firmly on the golf course only punctuated by lunches with local dignitaries and politicians, and seldom focused on events at the station.

"Come on, Brock, how was the man was murdered?!"

"He was stabbed in the chest, Sir," Brock answered blankly.

"You know what I mean, Brock," Tannock snapped. "How could anyone have killed the chap?!"

"I'm not sure yet, Sir," Brock answered, "but I'll find out."

Tannock eyed him for a moment before taking a deep breath. "Well, you better do it quickly. Now, to this other matter about Poole's mother."

"And his father, Sir," Brock interjected, "his father has now been taken as well."

Tannock leaned forward, resting his elbows on the desk, hands clasped before him.

"That's just it though, Brock. Sharp tells me there's no evidence that anyone's been 'taken', as you put it. By all accounts Poole's mother wasn't the most reliable sort, and his father is a known ex-criminal for heaven's sake! Involved in a drug gang, no less! I have to say, I might well have thought differently about young Poole coming to this station had I known."

Brock took a long, deep breath in order to calm the rage that was beginning to bubble inside him. When he answered, it was in a calm, clear tone, but one lined with steel.

"Sergeant Poole is a fine officer, and his family history doesn't effect that in any way. His parents have been taken by someone antagonistic to the family and it is clear that Sergeant Poole is their next target. We should be putting a security detail on him at all times, not denying the obvious just because there's no lead to go on. Whatever happened to looking after our own?" He rose from his chair and stared down at his superior officer.

"That's just the thing though isn't it, Brock?" Tannock said with a half-smile. "We look after our own, but sometimes we need to think carefully about who 'our own' includes exactly." He paused, and the air seemed to crackle between the two men in the silence. "I shall expect an update on this murder case soon. You can go." He looked down at some papers on the desk in front of him and studied them intently.

Brock turned and stormed from the room, realising that staying a moment longer might make him do something he would regret.

He marched down the corridor with his long stride and entered his office where Poole swivelled in his chair towards him as he took a seat in his own.

"Well, we've got something," Poole said, his voice trailing off as he saw the look on Brock's face. "Is everything alright, Sir?"

"We need to get to the bottom of this bloody case," Brock barked back angrily. "What have you got?"

"Well, London are working on handing Matty Heck back over to us, but they want to ask her a few questions at their end first."

"I hope you explained to them that a murder enquiry trumps any money laundering charge they might be trying to stick other?"

"I did, Sir," Poole answered, "but I don't think they plan to charge her at all."

"Go on," Brock asked with a raised eyebrow.

"It sounds like they're planning to make her flip on her clients and get her to give them details on their operations in exchange for witness protection."

Brock nodded thoughtfully. "And did they say anything about the business being gang related?"

"No, nothing," Poole said with a hint of frustration, "I asked about the retreat, but they said it wasn't on their radar at all."

"So this was maybe one of Matty Heck's legitimate business arrangements?" Brock said with a snort. "I don't believe it for a second, and that means that either Christopher Lake or Nora Russell have been involved in something dodgy enough to request her services."

"But why would that require them all to stay there?" Poole asked, "They told us it was because the retreat couldn't pay, but that doesn't make sense after looking at the financials of the retreat."

"Well we're only going to find out by talking to Matty Heck, I want her back up here pronto."

"They're calling back in an hour to give me an update on transporting her back here."

"Ok," Brock nodded. "I want to get back to the retreat as, apparently, we can't get them here."

"This window smasher in town?" Poole said standing, "Yeah, apparently the Chief Inspector has got half the force scrambled over it. Davies is on his own at the retreat but I called in Sanita to get over there as well."

"Then let's hope no one else tries to do a runner before she gets there, shall we?" Brock said standing up and moving around his desk towards the door. "I wouldn't trust Davies to stop a runner bean let alone a running murderer."

CHAPTER TWENTY-FIVE

B rock's phone blasted out The Dance of the Sugar Plum Fairy at top volume.

"Laura wants the baby to hear as much classical music as possible before it's born," he said by way of explanation to Poole who had turned from the road ahead to glance at him. "Hello?" Brock said as he placed the phone to his ear.

"Sam, it's Ronald Smith,"

"Do you have my lab results?"

"I do," the smug voice came down the line. "Where are you exactly? On the move, by the sounds of it."

"We're heading back to the retreat to talk to the suspects again."

"Oh, I thought you'd be heading into town to

take on this master criminal who has been smashing windows? A bit more on your level, maybe?"

"Just tell me the bloody results will you?" Brock snapped.

He gave a high chuckle, "I can see that this whole business is getting under your skin! Talking of which, let's start with the skin that was found under the victim's fingernails. I can confirm that it belonged to one of the guests at the retreat we tested, a Glenn Weaver. There was some blood there too, so I'd imagine he was scratched, which could have happened at the time of the stabbing."

"Excellent," Brock said. Feeling for the first time in this case that they really had something solid until he realised that the hair colour Ron had described from before would not match Glenn Weaver. "And the hair?" Brock continued.

"A match to Harold Olsen. Did you get anywhere with that receipt, by the way?"

"I traced it back to the shop, Rosa Briggs was the customer in question."

"Well it sounds like you have quite the range of suspects so I guess I better leave you to it, I must say that..."

Brock hung up as Ron began wittering on about what a challenging case it was. His mind was already elsewhere. Something Ron had said was bothering him.

"What did Ron have to say?" Poole said, breaking his train of thought. He related the news and added news of his trip to the shop where Rosa Briggs had bought a book on yoga.

"How on earth would a receipt get into his mouth?!" Poole asked, incredulous as he turned into the long driveway which led down to the retreat. "I mean, that doesn't happen in a struggle, does it? Do you think maybe the killer dropped it and he put it in his own mouth after the attack, you know, to point us to the killer?"

"No, Ron says he would have died almost instantly, which brings us to the other problem of all the jabs and cuts that were made around the wound after the initial stabbing."

"I would say it was to try to disguise the shape of the murder weapon," Poole said, "But that doesn't make sense because it was left in him."

"That's a good point," Brock said quietly. "Why didn't the killer take the knife with them and dispose of it?"

"Well, who knows? We don't even know how the killer got in and out of the room," Poole answered, exasperated. "In any case, the knife used was one everyone at the retreat had handled so it had all of their prints on it. Maybe the killer realised that?"

He pulled the car to a stop outside in the yard of the retreat and stepped out. "You ok, Sir?" he asked, leaning back in through the door to Brock who hadn't moved and was still sitting, gazing out of the window, his eyes unseeing.

"Yes, sorry," Brock blustered, clambering out with difficulty.

Brock was deep in thought as they made their way to the front door. There was something about this case that had been strange from the beginning. Parts of the case had fallen into place easily. They had motives and evidence in abundance, yet there was still the mystery of how someone could have committed the crime in the first place. The whole thing was a confusing mess, and those were the ones hated, where you couldn't see the wood for the trees.

"Afternoon, Sir," Davies said as the door opened to greet them as they approached.

"Everything alright here, Davies?"

"Um, well sort of, Sir," Davies said, his Adam's apple bobbing in his neck like a Yo-Yo.

"Oh, bloody hell, what's happened now?" Brock said, moving into the hallway and looking around.

"Nora Russell said they needed to order some food in as everyone was staying longer so I said it was fine for her to get home delivery, only she let the guests get whatever they wanted as an apology for being caught up in all this and…"

"And what, Constable? Out with it."

"Well, and now they've all had a bit to drink to tell you the truth, Sir. I didn't think I could really stop them."

"No problem Davies," he said, sighing with relief that something more awful hadn't happened. He clapped him on the shoulder and almost sent him into the wall on the far side of the hall, "If anything a little booze might loosen some tongues enough for us to make some progress. We'll set up in the office this time, I think," he said as he moved down the corridor which led into the right-hand wing of the extended farmhouse. The guests of the retreat were sitting in a small circle with cards laid out on a beanbag in the middle of them. Music played tinnily from someone's phone and there were numerous paper cups dotted around and a large bottle of rum was set on the floor. They looked up as they entered, and Glenn Weaver muttered something that caused the others to laugh.

"Where is Nora Russell?" Brock asked, noticing her absence from the group.

"She went to the bathroom," Davies replied.

Brock pushed open the door of the office to their left, which was slightly ajar and stepped inside.

"Wait outside a minute, Davies, and let me know when Miss Russell is back."

He looked around the room again as Poole came in behind him and closed the door behind him.

"What is it, Sir?"

"Oh nothing," Brock said distractedly as he gazed around the walls. "I don't suppose there's any chance we could have missed a secret passage by any chance is there?" he said with a sigh.

Poole moved around the room and began tapping on the walls, which all echoed with the same resonance.

"Can you hear their music, Poole?" Brock asked.

He watched his sergeant go still and tilt his head slightly. "Yes, just about. Why, Sir?"

"I was just wondering about the argument everyone supposedly heard. I was hoping that maybe this room was more soundproofed than it looked and that they might not have done."

"Why would they all lie though, Sir? They all said they heard the argument."

Brock turned to him. "It had crossed my mind that they could all be in on it," he said by way of explanation. "But then why would they even report it? There are plenty of places they could have just got rid of the body on the estate, somewhere in the grounds."

Brock regretted this choice of phrasing immediately as he saw the colour leave Poole's cheeks. It had obviously crossed his mind that the same fate could have befallen his mother.

"I'll be honest, Poole, I'm beginning to think that your mother isn't anything to do with this case at all." He sighed and leaned back on the desk. "I think there are only two possibilities in the death of Christopher Lake. That someone here killed him and everyone here is lying about it or what they saw, or that he was killed by someone from outside sneaking in. Now that person could be a rogue psycho, but that seems pretty unlikely from the neatness of the scene and leaving no apparent witnesses. So that leaves us with someone professional. Getting revenge for how he screwed them over in his previous life in the financial sector, maybe? If that was the case, what possible motive could they have for taking your mum? In any case, I don't see it for one reason. All the evidence that we've found on the other people here. I don't see how anyone from the outside could have arranged so much suspicion on others, and that's what I think some of this is, it's someone throwing suspicion around."

"Maybe Mum walked in on it happening? Maybe she saw something?" Poole said, his voice ice-cold.

"But then where are the witnesses? Someone here must have seen her arrive if that was the case. Anyway, they all heard Lake in here ranting and raving just before he was killed. That would hardly be at your mother, would it? And all of this lot have been here the whole time, apart from Matty Heck who we know went straight to London, so we know they couldn't have taken your father."

There was a moment of silence as Brock watched the hopeful news that his mother might not have been caught up in a murder enquiry clash with the realisation that their only possible lead might well come to nothing.

The door handle of the office turned, but the door stayed shut. There were some mumbled voices from outside before the door opened to reveal Nora Russell and Constable Davies.

"Sorry, Sir, couldn't get the door open," Davies said, "Miss Russell is here now."

"I can see that Davies, thank you," Brock answered wearily.

"You really must give us some idea of how long you expect us all to stay here," Nora said, folding her arms in front of her. "I have to begin to start making plans for the future of the company."

"And what are those plans?" Brock asked.

Nora's lips pursed. "Well, I've hardly had time to

even think about it with all this going on," she said bitterly.

"Why don't you go and have a think about it now while we talk to a few of your guests?"

She gave a harrumph, turned on her heel and made her way across to the group.

"Bring Glenn Weaver in will you, Davies?" Brock asked as he lowered himself into Nora Russell's desk chair.

"Yes, Sir," Davies said before scurrying off.

Poole dragged one of the two other chairs, which were against the wall across, as he had done before, and slumped into one in silence.

Brock glanced at him, but the faraway look in his eye that had been almost ever present over the last few days made him decide to not push his young colleague.

"Hello again," Glenn Weaver said in a cheery voice as he stepped into the office and slumped into the chair that faced them. "So, what is it this time?"

"We know that you had an affair with Matty Heck," Brock said leaning forward, "and that she then slept with Christopher Lake."

The ease with which the young man had entered the room, no doubt related to the rosy alcoholic glow in his cheeks, seemed to evaporate.

"I don't see what that's got to do with anything,"

he said in an annoyed tone. "We're all free agents," he shrugged.

"Are you? Does Rosa know that that's the situation?"

Glenn squirmed again. "Rosa and I are just casual," he answered.

"I see," Brock watched him for a moment. "Would you mind lifting up your shirt?"

"What?!" Glenn spluttered.

"It's a simple enough request, Mr Weaver. Could you please stand up, raise your shirt and turn around."

The young man swore but rose from his chair. "This has got to be against my rights or something," he muttered as he lifted his shirt.

"You're free to say no," Brock said watching as he turned slowly, "But then we'd have to take you down to the station and do things a bit more formally."

"Seen enough?" Glenn snapped as he dropped his shirt and slumped back in his chair.

Brock and Poole glanced at each other. There hadn't been a scratch on him that would account for the blood underneath the fingernail of the victim.

"Do you have any scratches or cuts on you, Mr Weaver?" Poole asked.

"Why? What on earth is this all about?" he answered angrily.

Poole glanced at Brock, who nodded. "We found traces of your skin and blood under the victim's fingernails."

Glenn Weaver's mouth opened, and then closed again. He looked between the two men, his eyes wide. "That's not possible," he said in a dry voice.

"I'll ask you again," Poole said. "Do you have any cuts on your body?"

Glenn gave a cold laugh as he shook his head. "This is ridiculous. The only cut on my body is here," he said, rolling up the right leg of his trousers to reveal a large square plaster. "So, unless you think I kneed him to death, can I get back to my card game?"

"How did you do it?" Brock asked.

"I tripped on the steps the other day, wasn't looking where I was going. The others can tell you and Nora filled out a bloody accident report and everything."

"Where did you get patched up?" Brock asked.

"Here," Glenn answered, a look of confusion crossing his face.

"Ok, you can go," Brock said. He watched Glenn leave and close the door hard behind him.

"Well, that's our big lead gone," Poole sighed in frustration.

"Maybe," Brock said. Something was stirring at the back of his mind, like an itch he couldn't quite reach. It was a feeling he had come to know well. He was on the right track somehow, he just needed to work out why.

"What is it, Sir?" Poole asked, his face alert with the sense that something had changed.

"I'm not sure yet," he answered before leaning down and peering into the metal wastepaper basket that was next to the desk. "Let's talk to Olsen about his hair being on the victim's clothing," he said thoughtfully as he rose back to an upright position in his seat.

CHAPTER TWENTY-SIX

"So Mr Olsen," Brock said in a light tone. "Can you think of any reason that we might have found one of your hairs on the victim's clothing?"

"My hair?"

"That's right Mr Olsen, your hair. I know you don't have much of it, but some of what you do have seems to have ended up on the victim."

Brock felt Poole's eyes flicker to him. No doubt wondering where this sudden improvement in mood had come from.

"I... I have no idea!" Olsen stammered. "It could have got on him from anywhere!"

"True, true," Brock said smiling. "Can I ask if you've noticed anything in your room being moved around at all?"

"In my room?" He blinked for a moment, staring

down at the desk in front of him. "Now you mention it, I did find my spare pair of glasses on the floor. It was strange as I know I'd left them in front of my dressing-table mirror and they were down the side by the wall. It took me ages to find them."

Brock looked at the neatly combed hair which ran around the side of the man's head. "And did you have a comb or a hairbrush on this dressing table?"

"Yes," Harold answered, looking completely bewildered by this line of questioning.

"Ok, thank you, Mr Olsen, that will be all for now," Brock said leaning back in his chair and watching the confused man leave the room.

"Am I missing something, Sir?" Poole asked once the door had closed again.

"Let's just run through everything we've found here," Brock said slowly. "We've got a group of people here on a work-related break right?"

"Right," Poole nodded.

"But with Matty Heck's business apparently a front for money laundering, I think we can safely say that the excursion here wasn't legit. So the first question to ask is, were Nora Russell and Christopher Lake in on it with her somehow?"

"Seems likely," Poole agreed.

"Now, we know that Rosa Briggs had had a moment with Lake and was put out when she found out that Matty Heck had slept with him, there could be motive there. Then there's Matty Heck herself, maybe something was going wrong in her business dealings with Lake, or maybe she just found out that Rosa had slept with him and lost it?"

"Ok," Poole said slowly, following the logic so far, but unsure of where it was going.

"But think about what evidence we have. First of all, there's the body itself. There was a single stab wound to the chest that punctured the heart and killed him almost instantly. Then there were other more superficial wounds that Ron thinks were made afterwards. Then we've got the fact that the murder weapon was a ceremonial knife that everyone here had touched, and then we find a hair on the victim's clothing that came from Harold Olsen and blood and skin cells under the fingernail that belonged to Glenn Weaver. That's a lot of evidence, don't you think?"

"It is, but none of it seems to make it any clearer who killed him," Poole answered.

"And why is that?" Brock asked, looking at Poole expectantly.

"Because all the suspects were outside this room and had a full view of the only entrance. It doesn't matter how much evidence we get, it's going to be impossible to find out who murdered him with all those witnesses saying that the thing couldn't have happened."

"Exactly!" Brock cried, laughing. "If we tried to pin this on any one of them, any defence lawyer worth her salt would be able to point to all the other potential suspects and say that it could have been them, and with us being unable to say how the crime was actually committed, the person we accuse would walk scot-free."

Poole frowned. "So, are you saying they really were all in on it together?"

"No," Brock answered, his face suddenly serious. "No, I think it was one of them alright. We've been trying to focus on motives. Normally that's the right thing to do, you start to poke around and eventually something clicks and you're set on a path to the truth. This case is different though. The problem has never been motive. The problem has always been how on earth could someone have been murdered in a room with a whole crowd of people outside the only entrance who all swear no one went in or out?"

"Well, yes," Poole said, confused by this covering of old ground.

"That's just it though," Brock said smiling. "They did see the killer enter the room."

"What?!"

"Not only that, they saw them leave again as well."

Poole shook his head, "I'm sorry sir, you've completely lost me on this one."

"You know what they say Poole, seeing is believing. I think it's time that we had a little demonstration for our captive audience, don't you?"

CHAPTER TWENTY-SEVEN

B rock surveyed the small group in front of him as they looked back in silence. The music had been turned off, their card game interrupted, and he now had their full attention. He had positioned himself against the back wall, facing out into the long room and forcing them all to turn away from the office behind them and towards him.

"Now I think you can all agree that this little business has been played out long enough," he said as he moved his gaze from eye to eye. "And I'm sure you would all like to go home."

"Bloody right," Glenn Weaver said bitterly.

"And so," Brock carried on, "I'd like you all to cooperate with us one more time and then I think we can put all this behind us."

"So you know who did it?" Rosa Briggs asked.

"We do," Brock said, his face becoming stern, his voice low. "We know that one of you murdered Christopher Lake."

"We've already told you," Glenn Weaver moaned, "It's not possible!"

"I'm glad you mentioned that," Brock said. "You know my colleague sergeant Poole and I have been interviewing in the office? Well, he is still in there and if you turn around now, you can see that I have asked Constable Davies to dress in one of Christopher Lake's robes and enter as Lake himself did on the day he died."

The group turned as one to see a white-robed figure, hood pulled up and covering his face. The figure lifted one hand in acknowledgement, before entering the office.

Brock watched the group carefully, his eyes lingering on one face slightly longer than the others. All of them looked shocked. The sight was clearly so similar to the one they had seen on that day.

"I take it from your faces that what you saw then was similar?" There were a few nods, but no one spoke. "Now, in a moment you should be able to hear Constable Davies and Sergeant Poole arguing." A few moments later, the sound of raised voices drifted across the room. "Can I ask if the volume is similar to the one you heard that morning?"

There was some shrugging from the group.

"Pretty much," Glenn Weaver answered, "but what is the point of all this?"

"I'm glad you asked," Brock said as one of the arguing voices fell silent and the door of the office opened. Poole stepped out and waited by the doorway as the group turned to him.

"If you'd all like to go and look in the office?" Brock said.

Glenn Weaver rose first and began making his way over with Rosa Briggs close behind him. Harold Olsen followed at a slower pace and Nora Russell was the last to rise and Brock followed her across the wooden floor.

Brock watched with pleasure as Davies' voice stopped its shouting before they reached the door and Glenn Weaver's face fell into a deep frown.

"What the hell?" he said, disappearing into the office.

The others gathered around the open doorway and peered into the empty office.

"But how the hell did he get out?" Glenn asked, turning back to them, his hands upturned in front of him.

"He didn't," Brock said, his eyes sparkling. "He was never in there in the first place."

"But we saw him go in!" Harold Olsen said, blinking back at him from behind his thick glasses.

"No you didn't," Brock said flatly. "You saw Poole here go in wearing the robe. I told you he was in there and you took as truth."

"But we heard him!" Rosa Briggs said.

"Look on the desk," Brock said to Glenn Weaver.

The young man turned and looked at the surface of the desk on his left where a silver Dictaphone lay. He reached out towards it and then stopped, turning back to Brock.

"It's ok, you can pick it up," he said. "Why don't you rewind a bit and play it back."

Weaver did so and the angry voice of Constable Davies shouted out from the small metal speaker grill at full volume. Weaver switched it off quickly.

"Well it's a clever little trick," Nora Russell said "But I don't see what it has to do with Christopher's death. We know he was in there."

"Oh, he was in there alright," Brock said, turning to her. "But he wasn't arguing with you was he, Miss Russell?"

"Of course he was," she snapped. "Don't be so ridiculous."

"You all saw Christopher Lake enter the office that morning, didn't you?" he said to the rest of them.

"Well, we thought we did," Glenn said, "But I'm

guessing what you're saying is, we saw someone else?"

"That's right, Mr Weaver," Brock said, "Maybe you should think about a career in the police force. No, I'm afraid that wasn't Christopher Lake that you all saw enter the office that morning, because he was already inside it, dead." Brock turned to Nora Russell whose pinched face had paled as this had played out in front of her. "You had already stabbed him, hadn't you Nora? My guess would be that it was early that morning before anyone else was up. I think it was a spur of the moment. Maybe you'd found out about something going on between Lake and Matty Heck? Whatever it was, you knew you had to cover up your involvement. You knew it wouldn't look like anything other than murder, so you needed to make sure that there were lots of suspects, lots of clues, in the hope that a good lawyer would be able to prove reasonable doubt if you faced a murder charge. You took it too far, though. You tried too hard. Let me run through what I think happened." Brock's eyes scanned the small gathering. Everyone was glued to him, hanging on his every word apart from Nora Russell herself, whose eyes gazed unfocused into the distance, a look of fear haunting her features.

"When everyone came down from their rooms to meet with Lake as they normally did, you weren't already in the office, you only entered it later dressed as Lake. From across the large room, they didn't notice that the figure was slightly smaller than the frame of Christopher Lake. You entered the room and then started the argument. But not a live one. It was a recording of the one you and Lake had already had. I don't know why you had chosen to record it. Maybe you were trying to get evidence of some kind against him? Whatever reason, you had it and used it. You played it, knowing that the last few bits of the argument had been Lake ranting at you without you replying, so when you left the office as you, everyone saw you leave. You had already stuffed the robe in his desk drawer so we would think it was just a spare of his, it was helpful that he always wore the same thing." He turned away from her to the others. "How long was it that you all said you had waited for Lake to come out of the office?"

"Two hours," Glenn replied, folding his arms. It seemed that he'd become the unofficial spokesman for the group who now all staring at Nora Russell. "But what the bloody hell was she doing all that time if she'd already killed him?!"

"Good question," Brock answered. "My guess is she panicked for a little while, but someone like you doesn't panic for long do you, Miss Russell?" He turned to her again and her eyes flickered up to him at the sound of her name.

"No, I think you used the time to plan. First of all, you went up to the bedrooms looking for something you could plant on the body to implicate someone else. Unfortunately for you, they were all locked, apart from two. Christopher Lake, who apparently operated an open door policy, and..."

"Mine!" Harold Olsen cried.

"That's right Mr Olsen, she went into your room and found a hair from your comb and that was the first bit of evidence she had. For the others, she had to get back in the office. She took a robe from Lake's room and pulled it on over her own clothes and simply walked back into the office in front of you all. Then she removed the knife she had used to stab him and replaced it with the ceremonial knife that was in Lake's drawer because she knew it would have everyone's prints on. She made sure to wiggle it about enough, hoping to disguise the difference of the blow that killed him. Next, she added a little of your DNA under the victim's fingernails, Mr Weaver."

"But how the hell did she do that?!" The young man cried angrily.

"From the cut on your knee," Brock answered. "She'd cleaned up your cut in this very office and all she needed to do was to scoop some of your blood and tissue from the tissue in the bin and push it under Lake's fingernail. Once she'd done that, she played the argument on the Dictaphone and walked out as Nora Russell again a few minutes later with the real murder weapon hidden on her somewhere. In the time you were all waiting, she got rid of it somehow. How am I doing, Nora?" He turned to her. Her expression had changed from the pale and worried look that had haunted her earlier to something harder, more determined. As he had suspected, Nora Russell was a woman who found solutions to problems, even if that meant murder. So did she have a new plan? Or had she accepted her fate?

"Do you have anything to say?" he prompted.

"Only that you're right," she said in a matter-of-fact manner, "but I had no choice. It was self-defence. And I'd do it again."

"That's something for the court to decide," Brock answered. "For now, you're under arrest. We will take your statement back at the station. Read her her rights, Poole."

Poole opened his mouth to begin, but Nora continued before he could speak. "I have something to show you before you take me to the station."

CHAPTER TWENTY-EIGHT

Brock held on to the cool steel of the frame as Poole pressed the accelerator and they headed off across the grass and away from the yard. They were sitting in the small golf buggy that had been behind one of the outbuildings. Poole driving, Nora Russell in handcuffs next to him in the passenger seat, and Brock perched on the back shelf that had been converted to haul garden equipment. The tailgate was down and he had doubled up a dust sheet that had been folded on the back seat under him, but the vibrations were still making his teeth rattle. Nora Russell was taking them to where she had disposed of the murder weapon, but her expression and manner had him worried.

"You say it was self-defence," he said above the

whine of the small electric engine. "Did Lake attack you?"

She half turned to him and nodded. "As I told you before, Christopher had the capital and I had the location and the business acumen. At first, it was a good partnership, and we got this place up and running and asking good money. You'd be amazed how many financial businesses will pay to get their workforce some relaxation."

"Lake used his contacts in the industry?"

"He did at first, but it quickly became a word-of-mouth thing. Once a few companies had used us and word got around the city, everyone wanted to come."

Brock redoubled his grip as they went over a bump in the grass, which almost sent him toppling off the vehicle.

"Sorry, Sir," Poole said from the driving seat, "didn't see it."

Brock grunted and looked off into the distance. They were heading for a copse of trees in a dip towards the edge of the grounds of the estate. It was still some distance away, and the buggy wasn't the fastest vehicle in the world.

"So what changed?" he asked, continuing this mobile interrogation. He watched Nora's lips purse and wriggle in that way she had that made it look as though she was chewing on a wasp.

"I discovered that Christopher was keeping... unusual company. We were having visits from people that were nothing to do with the retreat and Christopher would have meetings with them without me. I suspected there was some sort of illegal activity going on that I was unaware of and confronted him about it. He denied everything, but he made it very clear that my place was just to look after the business side of the retreat and not to stick my nose into anything else. After that, things went downhill. I was always trying to find out what was going on. He was becoming more secretive and more bad-tempered. And then, on the day he died, I told him I was going to quit, and that I wanted my share back out of the business."

Brock eyed her carefully. Although situated behind her on the buggy, he had positioned himself on the right so he could see her face in profile. From what he could see, she was almost expressionless. She gazed out ahead of them towards the approaching tree line and talked as though she was reading the information from the back of a cereal packet rather than discussing how she ended the life of her business partner.

"He went into a rage, screaming and shouting at me that I could never leave, that he wouldn't let me. He came at me and grabbed me around the throat. I could see his eyes that he was going to kill me, I just panicked. I was against his desk and he had a silver letter opener that his old firm had given him when he'd left. I grabbed it and stabbed him. I didn't mean to kill him, I just wanted to get him off of me. I realised what I'd done and ran out of there. I panicked, I didn't think anyone would believe me so I thought I'd confuse things for you. It was the recording that actually gave me the idea. I'd started recording some of our arguments in case I could use them in any court case that might happen. I realised I could use it to give myself an alibi if I made it appear that Christopher was still alive when everyone saw me leave the office."

She fell silent and Brock considered her words carefully as Poole brought the buggy to a stop.

"We found Lake sitting in his chair, behind the desk," he said quietly in the sudden silence which filled the small cab as the whine of the buggy's engine shut down.

Nora turned to him with a sharp, jerky movement. "I moved him," she said simply before stepping off of the vehicle. Poole turned in his seat and gave Brock a raised eyebrow look that said he found all this a little strange too.

There was another problem that was running through Brock's mind as he jumped down from the back of the buggy with a thud and a stretch of his back. The buggy ride to this far edge of the estate had taken ten minutes. Why had Nora Russell used her precious time in between having to return to play the part of Christopher Lake to drive the murder weapon out here? Yes, she needed to get rid of it, but was this really the first place she had thought of? Maybe she had not been thinking straight and had just jumped on the buggy? Whatever the reason, the skin on the back of his neck had begun to tingle, a sure sign that somewhere in his brain alarm bells were ringing. He just wished he knew what they meant.

Nora Russell had already begun walking towards the trees, where a narrow line where the grass had been worn down indicated a path. Although it only appeared to be no more than a few hundred feet long in either direction, the trees were densely packed and almost as soon as they entered the light dimmed to a low gloom.

"There's another outbuilding here?" Poole said from the middle of the single file line of three.

Brock looked up and peered past them. Just through the trees, he could make out the faded wooden slats of a building.

"Yes, that's where I hid the letter opener," Nora said.

This didn't make sense to Brock. Why would you

hide the murder weapon in a building? Buildings got searched, they invited inspection by their very nature. It would be much better to have thrown the letter opener into a nearby bush where, on an estate this size, it may never be found.

"Stop," he called out urgently. The others stopped and turned to him. Poole had a look of concern on his face, Nora's expression was more worrying. She looked calm, with an air of almost self-satisfied smugness about her. "Just what the hell is going on here?" Brock growled at her.

"I think, Inspector Brock," said a deep voice from his right, "that I may be able to help with that."

All three of them turned to see a man step out from behind a tree, a thin smile on his lips, and a gun in his hand.

CHAPTER TWENTY-NINE

Brock stared at the man in disbelief. Whatever he had thought was going on with Nora Russell, he hadn't been expecting this. An accomplice. He glanced to his left and saw Poole's expression. He was wide-eyed and pale, taking a step back as though a physical blow had landed on him. Brock's gaze jerked back to the man and then back to Poole as he realised with a shock that Poole seemed to recognise the man.

"Alfie?" Poole croaked, his voice sounding like the dry branches underfoot.

"So you recognise me?" The man said with the same amused tone that he had spoken previously. "I wondered if you would."

Poole reached into his pocket and pulled out the small cube that he had kept on his person since he had found it in his flat. He stared at it for a moment and then looked up at the man.

"Where are they?"

"Ah," the man laughed. "I can see you're keen for a family reunion. Well, all in good time. Why don't we move inside where we can have more of a chat?" He gestured with the gun.

For the first time, Poole's eyes left the man as he glanced at Brock. His eyes were still wide, but now there was something other than surprise there. Confusion? Anger? Brock couldn't tell. What he did know was that whoever this man was, he had affected Poole hugely, and in a way, he hadn't seen before.

Poole and Brock turned towards the barn and began moving as Nora Russell stepped to one side, her arms folded and a smile on her face.

"You too, Nora," the man said in a cold tone.

She spun towards him in shock.

"What?!" she cried angrily. "You promised me! We had a deal!"

"And just like your deal with Lake, things change," the man shrugged with a slight chuckle. He gestured with the gun again towards the barn. For a moment, Brock wondered whether Nora was going to rush at him. She glared for a moment, a quiet fury clearly visible before she turned and walked towards the building. She had obviously realised that the distance between them could never be covered before he had fired.

The three of them trudged towards the barn, following the thin path that wound around to the opposite side where a small clearing in the trees was marked out with a row of large stones. The barn's doors were made of the same faded and warped wood that made up the rest of the building. They were closed, but a dim, flickering light appeared around the cracks.

"Nora," the man said, "why don't you do the honours, and let us in?"

Nora scowled at him, but moved forward and opened the doors with some difficulty, the bottom of them scraping on the dirt floor where they had dropped on their ancient hinges.

"Inside, and stand on the right-hand side," the man said, gesturing again with the gun.

Brock followed Nora and Poole into the gloom and flinched as he heard his sergeant gasp.

"Mum!" Poole shouted and ran to the left-hand corner of the barn where Jenny Poole was sitting on an upturned cart. Her hands were tied in front of her and a strip of cloth had been wound around her head and into her mouth as a gag. Poole pulled it from her as he knelt in front of her and she gasped for air as tears rolled down her cheeks.

"I'm fine Guy, I'm ok," she sobbed as he embraced her.

"Not much good at following orders is he, Inspector Brock?" the man said, "That's probably something you should work on, Guy?"

Poole spun towards him. "You let her go right now, Alfie," he shouted. "You've got me here now, you don't need her as well."

"Well, that's where you're wrong, Guy, isn't it?" Alfie said with a hard edge to his voice that made Brock nervous. It was the tone of someone who would be willing to fire the gun that rested in his hand. Brock and Nora had followed Alfie's instructions and were against the right-hand wall of the small barn. His eyes scanned the place looking for any sign of Jack Poole, but there was none. Where was he? A sick feeling began to grow in his stomach.

"You see," Alfie continued, "I do need all of you. I need the whole Poole family. I want everyone who played a part in that day to pay just like Simon did."

Brock's mind whirred. He knew that Simon was the name of the boy who had died when the Poole family home had been shot at all those years ago, only now did he remember the name of the other boy. It was Alfie.

"You were there on that day?" he said, hoping to

pull the man's attention away from Poole and his mother.

"Ah, and at last the Inspector has caught up to the day's events," Alfie said with a grin. "Yes, Inspector. I was there that day. I was there to watch my best friend die in front of me and my other friend get shot, but it wasn't just that day for me." His eyes grew cold as he talked. "I was in the room watching my friends get shot every day after that. Well, every night. I dreamed of it, couldn't stop. I started to fear to go to sleep because I knew what would be coming. My family moved us away after the incident. Wanted to get me away from the bad influences I'd clearly fallen under. So I lost my friends, my home, my whole life. I was a good kid, I didn't deserve that."

"I was just a kid, too," Poole growled at him as he rose from his mother's side and turned to face Alfie. "It affected us too, you know!"

"Oh, I know it did," Alfie laughed. "Your dad in prison, your mum a loon always looking for the next spiritual voodoo solution to her problems, and then there's you, Guy." He took a step towards Poole and folded his arms, the gun still resting lightly in his hand. "You used it to improve yourself, right the wrongs of the world, is that it?" He cocked his head on one side.

"I just tried to get on with my life," Poole answered angrily.

"Ah, well that's the key, isn't it?" Alfie sneered. "Some of us didn't get the choice to get on with our lives. Some of us were stuck in that day forever!" He raised the gun at Poole and Brock felt the panic rise in his chest.

"Where is Jack Poole?!" he boomed, making Alfie turn to him.

"Oh!" Alfie laughed. "Haven't you seen him yet?" He grinned at Brock, a malevolent, thin smile.

"Guy," Jenny Poole said croakily, "over there," she nodded to the right-hand corner of the barn where a pile of old sacking lay. "He hurt him, Guy," she sobbed as Poole moved across to the pile. Brock kept one eye on Alfie as Poole moved across to the pile. He was clearly enjoying this. For now, he wasn't going to shoot. He wanted to pile maximum pain on Poole first.

Poole knelt down and pulled the top two sacks from the pile and threw them to one side. Jack Poole lay there, his eyes closed, blood smeared across his face. His hands and feet were tied.

There was a moment of silence as Poole checked his pulse.

"I hope he's still alive," Alfie said. "I want him to watch all this as I had too."

"You bastard," Poole growled, standing and spinning towards Alfie again. "Why are you doing this? It's not going to change anything that happened, it's not going to make things better!"

"You think this is about making things better?" Alfie said. There was still a smile on his lips, but it had hardened now into something humourless.

"Then what the hell is it?" Poole roared, his arms waving around him at the small gathering of people who were standing in silence.

"It's about making sure that the people responsible for ending Simon's life, for ending my life, pay," Alfie said with a quiet ferocity. "I'm going to make sure that the three of you get what you should have had coming to you ten years ago. I'm going to make sure you all die."

CHAPTER THIRTY

There was a period of thick silence that seemed to seep out and spread around the barn like a thick fog. Brock took a slow deep breath as he assessed the situation. The man with the gun was too far away from any of them to be rushed, he would have fired before any of them laid a finger on him. Jenny Poole was still sitting in the left-hand corner, her eyes fixed on her son and the unmoving figure of her ex-husband. Poole looked as though he was considering charging at Alfie, if for no other reason than blind rage. His fists clenched and unclenched at his side, and his chest heaved with short, shallow breaths. Brock knew he needed to calm his young partner down. This Alfie seemed to be hell-bent on exacting some kind of revenge and it didn't seem like he needed any more reasons to get started. Brock had already decided that this was no idle threat. Alfie had already kidnapped two people and clearly had some sort of involvement in the murder of Christopher Lake. Brock glanced to his right at Nora Russell who was standing next to him. Since being ordered to move into the barn along with Brock and Poole, she had been quiet. Her eyes narrowed. He decided that the best thing that could happen now was for some of the attention to be taken off Poole.

"So you're Nora's partner, are you?" he said loudly, causing the gunman's gaze to shift towards him.

"Partner?" Alfie laughed. "I'm not her partner! Dear me, Inspector Brock, I had a rather higher opinion of you than that."

Brock shrugged. "She obviously found this location," he said gesturing at the barn. "And I'm guessing she was the one to get Lake out of the way so you could use it. What exactly have you brought to the party?"

Alfie's face moved from an initial flash of anger to one of confusion. "You think I needed them? You think I needed anyone?! Nora here is a fool."

"I held up my end of the deal!" Nora shouted suddenly, stepping forward. "You're the one who's not kept your word!" She folded her arms and glared at him indignantly as Alfie stared back with an almost amused expression. "I think you're forgetting that I know things about you, so perhaps you'd better start treating me with more respect."

The noise of the gun firing was so loud in the barn that for a few seconds afterwards, Brock could hear nothing. He raised his hands to his ears and pushed his fingers against them as he stared around. Poole had stumbled back to sit next to his father and for a brief moment, Brock's heart seemed to skip a beat until he realised his partner had not been hit. It was Nora, clutching at her chest, who fell backwards next to him, her eyes wide and already rolling into the back of her head. He bent down next to her, but the amount of blood that poured through her fingers as she clasped the wound meant he knew it was too late.

"Well, that's one less thing to worry about," Alfie said in a flat tone. "And while we wait for Poole senior to wake up, let's take a moment to talk about that pathetic excuse for a woman," he sneered. "You're wrong on almost every point, Inspector. I decided on this location, partly because I knew that Nora Russell was talking to Matty Heck about helping with the money laundering business, and partly because when I met her it was obvious she was one of the most greedy people I had ever met in my life. This Lake character you mention was some slimeball from the city, but according to Nora, he had started to believe his own mumbo-jumbo about all this spirituality nonsense. He wanted no part of the money laundering and he wanted Nora out. Obviously, she had other ideas and asked me to," he paused and gave a sickly smile, "help her with that little problem." Both Jenny and Guy Poole were still, Brock looked down at Nora again and knew with a sickening certainty that she was dead. He cursed mentally and got up, facing Alfie again.

"So you killed Lake?"

Alfie laughed bitterly. "No, Nora apparently lost her temper and decided to take matters into her own hands. She called me in a panic and I gave her some pointers about how to give you the run around inspector, I hope you enjoyed the game?"

"We still solved it," Brock answered.

"You were meant to Inspector! I had told the silly bitch that if you got onto her she should lead you down here and I'd take care of it." He sighed and shook his head, looking down at the body. "For all of her conniving nature, she really was quite stupid, you know. She actually thought I was going to help her get away with murder."

"And instead you were just using her," Brock said flatly.

"Of course, she was a means to an end. She gave

me access to this location, and more importantly, she gave me access to Guy here," he turned back towards the sergeant. "You know, Inspector? We were all good friends back in the day, but Simon and I were closer. He lived just two doors down from me and we were like brothers." His eyes grew narrow and cold. "I had to watch his parents deal with their loss, watch his little sister crying in the street. I had to watch as they lowered him into the ground."

"None of us can change what happened," Poole said, his voice hoarse with emotion. "I'd do anything to bring Simon back, but all we can do is try to live our lives in a way that he would have wanted."

"That he would have wanted?!" Alfie roared. "How the hell would you know what he wanted? He was only fifteen! All any of us wanted was the latest computer game and for some girl to notice us. He wasn't thinking about how he wanted us to live his life when your family's actions got him killed!"

Jack Poole stirred by Poole, who turned to look at him. "Dad?" he said softly.

"Ah, good, now the whole gang is here," Alfie said with a malicious sneer.

As Alfie and Jenny focused on watching Poole help his father upright, Brock edged slowly away from the wall of the barn and towards Alfie. He had moved a good few feet before the gunman's head jerked to the right and the nozzle of the gun followed it to swing around and point at Brock's stomach.

"What exactly is your plan here?" Brock said, spreading his palms out facing upwards. "The main manor is still a crime scene, and there are uniformed officers there who will be following along any minute once they realise we've been away too long."

"Oh, really? I heard that your resources were slightly stretched today? Meaning there is only one uniformed officer here at the moment?"

Brock nodded in realisation. "You arranged for the windows to be smashed in town."

"The problem with Her Majesty's finest is that they are so bloody predictable," Alfie laughed. "Your Chief Inspector spends more time at the golf course and his gentlemen's club than he does at home or work, it wasn't hard to see what would grab his attention." His attention turned back to Guy and Jack, now sitting side by side. Jack was breathing heavily, the left-hand side of his face a swollen mess of dried blood and bruising.

"Hey!" Alfie shouted, "No talking at the back of the class, or perhaps you'd like to share with everyone what you were saying?"

Guy stopped the hushed tones with which he had been conversing with his father and got up. "Alfie, you said it yourself. We were friends," he said as he took a step towards him. "We grew up together, you don't want to do this. Just put down the gun and we can figure all this out."

Brock watched the expression on Alfie's face. Poole was trying the only thing he could think of to delay, to get himself in front of his parents, but it wasn't going to work.

Why had Alfie wanted to wait for Jack to wake up? Brock had known with a sickening feeling as soon as the young gunman had said it. He wanted to kill Guy in front of his parents. He wanted them to watch their son die just as he had watched his friend Simon die, and now Poole was moving towards him.

Brock thought of Laura. Her kind, but mischievous, eyes that always seemed to dance with life. The way she constantly teased him and played jokes on him, but always ended them with a playful kiss. Then he thought of the life they had created that was only just growing inside her.

Even as these images and thoughts flashed across his mind, he was moving. Launching himself forward towards Alfie with a bellowing roar, ensuring that the gunman turned to him and away from his sergeant. The figure in front of him turned, a look of complete shock on his face as a loud crack rang out in the barn and Brock felt something akin to ice spread from the inside of his right shoulder. He continued without slowing, smashing into the figure as another loud crack rang out as they fell to the floor. Brock landed heavily on top of Alfie as a similar feeling of ice spread from the right side of his stomach.

He bounced to one side as he heard shouts from what he could have sworn was Davies' voice before a dull thud and grunt as a weight landed across him. He opened his mouth to call Poole's name as the dim light in the barn began to fade, but no sound left his lips. His last thought as darkness enveloped his vision and consciousness slipped from his mind, consisted of just three words.

The cursed detective.

CHAPTER THIRTY-ONE

B rock opened his eyes with some effort. His eyelids seemed to be glued together, and it required several rapid blinks before they freed and vague shades of white appeared in front of him. There were voices, too, but just like the outlines that bobbed across his vision, they too remained muffled and unclear. Then he felt a hand on his cheek and felt a wave of relief as he realised that Laura was with him.

CHAPTER THIRTY-TWO

Two days later, Brock was sitting in his hospital bed and stared out of the window. His right arm hung limply in a sling, his stomach was strapped in what seemed to be an endless array of bandaging. He hadn't had the stomach to look at either of his wounds when the nurse had changed his dressing this morning, but he was told that he was "doing well", which sounded like good news.

So far he had only seen Laura after waking from the surgery that had removed the bullet that had lodged in his shoulder, the one which had entered his side passing clean through without hitting anything vital. He had been lucky. As Laura had hugged him and kissed his forehead, tears of relief rolling down her cheeks, he had been overcome by an incredible sense of guilt. He had made the decision to put himself at risk, he had run at Alfie knowing full well that it might mean his child would grow up without a father, that his wife Laura would be a single parent before she'd even started, and still he'd run. He'd made that decision, and Laura must know it. He had half expected her to slap him, instead, she held him, and they sobbed together.

It was only later that she spoke of the incident. Telling him that he was a brave idiot, she told him she was proud of him, causing him to tear up again. He decided the tears must have been a side effect of the anaesthetic they had used during his operation.

Now he was waiting for Poole. He closed his eyes and exhaled slowly as he thought again how lucky they had all been. No one else had been injured, no one else had been killed.

The door opened, and he turned to see Poole's gangly frame step through with a wide grin across his face.

"Hello, Sir," he said as he moved across to the bed. "Finally decided to wake up then?"

"I'd be back at home if they'd bloody let me," Brock grumbled, shifting his position slightly and arranging a cushion to prop himself up. "We seem to be making a habit of ending up in hospital, don't we, Poole?" He smiled.

"We do, Sir, but I guess that's the price we pay for being such brave heroes."

Brock swore. "So you've seen the paper then?"

Poole nodded, still grinning. "Very flattering photo of you I thought, Sir,"

"And I don't suppose you know how they ended up hearing what happened in that barn, do you?"

Poole's face went to stone. "No idea at all, Sir," he answered blankly.

"Well, I think it's pretty clear," Brock said as he lifted the paper from his lap. "There was another hero on the day, young constable David Davies who bravely apprehended the armed killer after the Inspector had been wounded." Brock looked back at Poole and raised one eyebrow.

"Well," Poole shrugged, "it is true, Sir. Davies came in just after Alfie fired and whacked him over the head with a milk churn as he tried to get up."

"How did he know where we were?"

"He followed the tracks of the golf buggy apparently, you could see where it had gone on the wet grass."

Brock frowned thoughtfully. "But why did he even follow us in the first place? Don't tell me he figured out that something was wrong before we did."

Poole laughed. "No, Sir, apparently he'd had a

call to head into town because there were more windows being smashed and he wanted to check with you before he left the other guests back at the retreat."

"These window smashers, did we catch them?"

"Yes, Sir, just a few kids that Alfie had paid to throw stones. It seems he offered them twenty pounds for every window smashed so they got a bit... enthusiastic." Poole smiled and then his face grew more serious. "I want to say thank you, Sir. You saved my life."

Brock sighed. "I don't know, Poole, maybe I made him shoot."

"No," Poole said quickly, shaking his head. "I hadn't kept a lid on my emotions and he was going to shoot me, I know it." He looked down. "That wasn't the Alfie I knew. I think he was telling the truth when he said he died as well as Simon the day of the shooting."

"And he's in custody, he's been processed?"

Poole nodded. "Sharp and Anderson have interviewed him, apparently he's quite talkative." He looked at Brock sharply. "Still threatening me and my family, apparently."

"He won't be able to do anything where he's going," Brock growled. "How is Jack? Laura said he's healing well?"

"He's fine," Poole smiled. "Says he had worse when he was inside, but I think he was joking."

"Has he explained what happened when Alfie took him?"

"You were right," Poole answered, "When he went to your flat he went alone, he didn't want to turn up to your home with hired goons, apparently. Anyway, he noticed someone following him and decided to let them take him. He thought he could get to Mum that way. Alfie was obviously aware of the threat though, because as soon as he got him back to the barn he hit him over the back of the head and gave him a whack every time he came around." Poole's voice tailed off and there was a moment of silence before he continued again. "Mum's still quite shaken, she's gone to stay with Ricardo for a few days."

Brock raised an eyebrow.

"I know!" Poole laughed, "I think there might actually be something real there."

Brock chuckled and then winced as his side erupted in pain.

"Are you ok, Sir?" Poole asked, his face full of concern.

"Fine," Brock grumbled. He hated this. He felt weak and useless, stuck in this bed with matching holes in his shoulder and side. "So this Alfie, he was your friend when you were younger?"

Poole nodded, his face suddenly looking drawn and tired. "We were in the same class at school together. Me, Simon, and Alfie. We did everything together, but Simon and Alfie were always closer as they lived on the same street. On my birthday," he paused and swallowed, making Brock feel guilty for making him relive this, "On the day it happened, the three of us were there together playing a game. Alfie was the only one of us who didn't get shot. He never visited me in hospital, he never came back to school, his family moved away a month or two later. They'd written a letter to Mum saying that we were not to contact them again." He shrugged. "They were just trying to protect him."

"But at the same time they removed him from everything he knew," Brock interjected, "and right after a traumatic event like that as well, you've got to wonder what that would do to a young lad."

"Well, now I think we know," Poole said solemnly. They both paused for a moment as they reflected on this.

"Nora Russell died while in our custody," Brock said quietly. The thought had been gnawing at him since he had woken. No matter what type of person she was, no matter what she had done, once they had arrested her she should have been able to rely on their protection. She had died in handcuffs, and part of the blame had to be on them.

"They've already started an internal investigation," Poole said.

Brock looked up at him sharply. "Have you spoken to them yet?"

"No," Poole answered shaking his head, "A woman is apparently arriving tomorrow, she'll be staying in Bexford until the matter is resolved. I don't think there was anything we could have done, though, he had a gun, and we didn't."

Brock nodded. He had seen enough of internal affairs to know that it wasn't always about what you could have done differently, sometimes it was about your decision making. He knew they had made a mistake by allowing Nora Russell to take them out to that barn, he also knew that his team should have found the barn when they had done their initial search of the area. Oh, he had excuses. The team was small and the barn well hidden, Nora Russell had confessed and was leading them to the murder weapon. Whether that would fly with internal affairs was another matter, though.

"When I get out of here," he said, deciding to think of happier things, "I want the whole team down at The Mop & Bucket and I don't want anyone to leave sober. I might even buy the first round."

Poole grinned at him. "If I mention that the whole station will turn up."

Brock frowned. "On second thoughts, it's probably customary for the person whose life has been saved to buy the first round, to show gratitude."

Poole rolled his eyes and got up. "I'll see you later, Sir."

"Bye, Poole, thanks for coming."

Brock watched him go and felt a wave of emotion flood through his body. He realised with a shock that he was crying. He raised his hand to wipe away the tears and saw that it shook. He had almost died, and Poole had almost died. His child almost grew up without ever seeing his face, without ever being held by him.

He lay back on his pillow and wept.

CHAPTER THIRTY-THREE

The late evening light filtered through the filthy window like warm butter, which only added to Brock's feeling that he was in a frying pan. He reached up and wiped his forehead as he watched Chief Inspector Clive Tannock read through the letter in front of him. After what seemed like an age, he looked up.

"Well, I have to say that this is a surprise, Brock. I always had you pegged as someone who'd rather be out on the street than behind a desk."

"Things change, Sir, and I think there will be opportunities to keep my hand in."

Tannock raised an eyebrow at this. "Really? Well, I'm sure you know best. You know that Inspector Sharp is also being considered for this role?"

"I do, Sir," he said flatly, resisting the urge to say what he really thought of Inspector Sharp. A man who was so engrossed in his own, small, petty version of the world that he failed to pay any attention to the real one that washed past him like water around a stone. His ridiculous moustache, his blinkered view of police work (and life in general now Brock came to think of it), annoyed Brock every time he saw the man, so he generally tried not to.

"Well," Tannock continued with a sigh. "Sharp withdrew his name from the running this morning, so I would be happy to recommend you officially as my replacement."

Brock was sitting in an ice-cold well of silence.

"Sharp withdrew?"

"Yes, that's what I said. He decided in light of recent events," he cleared his throat and shuffled the papers in front of him, "that it was time for his retirement as well."

Brock tried to process this unexpected information, but his brain was too overwhelmed by the other large and looming thought that was bursting around his brain. He was being recommended to be the next Chief Inspector.

He and Laura had talked long into the night. They had discussed their future, their soon-to-be-born child, their new and uncertain future as a family. He knew it was the right decision, deep in his bones, and certainly every time in the last few weeks that the gunshot wound in his shoulder itched, and yet...

He was gripped with a sudden fear, a fear that he would lose his edge and become like the man who was sitting in front of him. Greyed, sagging around the middle with a nose whose red glow spoke of fine whiskey and an obsession with the golf course rather than the station and its work.

"You have only just been declared fit for work again after your..." Tannock hesitated over mentioning the shooting, "... incident, and so I don't expect you to do much other than paperwork for a while." He looked up at Brock and gave a thin smile. "But then that will be good practice, won't it? Dismissed."

Brock stared for a moment at the top of his superior's head as it bent to the papers in front of him again before rising from his seat and turning to the door, his mind blank. He walked down the corridor towards the main office as though on auto-pilot. No thoughts whirled around his head. Just an icy calm that if anything was more terrifying than panic. When he opened the door, he heard the familiar warm buzz of people working and chatting and his mind, suddenly, woke again.

Poole was sitting on the edge of Sanders' desk and laughed with her as Constable Davies said something, no doubt relating the most recent disastrous episode of his eventful love life.

No, thought Brock, he wouldn't become like Tannock. These people deserved better, this station deserved better, and he was going to make sure they got it.

He strode over to them and hoisted his trousers up. "Right you lot, I think it's pretty clear that we have all forgotten something important."

The laughter stopped as they turned to him and saw the serious expression his face held.

"Sir?" Poole said, rising from the desk and onto his feet.

"I'm waiting for one of you to tell me what it is, Poole," Brock answered, folding his arms. The three of them looked at each other, Davies swallowed and his Adam's apple performed its usual gymnastics.

"There is one vital task that I had hoped the three of you would never forget, bearing in mind how vital it is to us all."

Now they looked worried. They weren't looking at each other now, they were looking at him, their eyes wide and their brows furrowed.

He walked past them towards reception and called over his shoulder "And because you have forgotten that we always visit the pub after closing a case, all three of you will be buying the first rounds."

He allowed himself a small smile as he pushed the door open to reception, hearing the scrabble of footsteps behind him as they followed at pace.

MAILING LIST

Get FREE SHORT STORY *A Rather Inconvenient Corpse* by signing up to the mailing list at agbarnett.com

Made in the USA
Middletown, DE
22 March 2021

35999613R00130